THIRD KNOCK THE CHARM

Eastwind Witches 3

NOVA NELSON

FFS
≡ MEDIA ≡

ISBN: 978-0-9996050-7-3 (FFS Media)

Previously published as *Third Knock the Charm: Witches of Salem, A Nora Bradbury Paranormal Cozy Mystery 3*

Cover Design © FFS Media LLC

Cover design by Molly Burton at cozycoverdesigns.com

Third Knock the Charm, Eastwind Witches #3 / Nova Nelson -- 1st ed.

www.novanelson.com

Contents

THIRD KNOCK THE CHARM

Eastwind Witches 3

NOVA NELSON

Chapter One

✦❦✦

"This would be illegal a year ago," Tanner Culpepper said as our small group entered Ezra's Magical Outfitters.

"Why's that?" I asked, passing Tanner as he held open the door. Ruby True, the only other Fifth Wind witch in Eastwind, outside of myself, had come along to offer advice, and took her time entering behind me. Our familiars brought up the rear—Clifford, Grim, and, riding on Grim's back, Tanner's familiar, Monster. As a munchkin cat, she spent her days in Eastwind in a nervous state, what with all the werewolves and shapeshifters running around. The only way we could get her to go anywhere outside of the house was if she rode on Grim.

"The Council had strict laws for a long time," Tanner explained, finally able to let go of the door once our veritable parade had entered. "Witches weren't allowed to get our wands until after we'd graduated from Mancer Academy and joined the Coven. Seems the Council wasn't big on a bunch of untrained witches running around with wands, so they outlawed it."

Ruby leaned toward me as we paused in the entrance of the brightly lit shop. "Didn't stop me from getting one," she said.

"You never went through the formal schooling?" I asked.

"What do those idiots have to teach a Fifth Wind witch? There wasn't a single one like me when I came to town. I can read books well enough to teach myself the basic spells. The rest was just a matter of listening to my Insight."

I decided not to point out that when I'd suggested learning on my own, Ruby had snuffed out that possibility as soon as it'd left my mouth. Do as I say, not as I do was Ruby's go-to. But she did insist that she would be a good enough teacher for me, and that the Coven had nothing particularly useful to teach me. So, I hadn't bothered applying for Mancer Academy.

Ezra Ares, the young and friendly owner of Ezra's Magical Outfitters who always had a twinkle in his eyes and a furtive grin resting on his lips, waved at us as we entered. As Ruby shuffled over to speak with him where he stood behind a glass U-shaped display case, Tanner took my hand and led me farther into the store to browse the selection.

Instinctively, though, I scanned the store to make sure no one we knew was nearby and saw us together. Tanner taking my hand was innocuous enough—he could just be getting my attention—except I knew it wasn't.

Because Tanner and I had been secretly dating for two weeks now.

Well, it seemed like dating. We hadn't labeled it anything. But after the kiss we shared in the office of Medium Rare, just after we'd made it official with co-owning the diner, there was little gray area about what was happening between us.

It *felt* like a happily ever after. But don't worry, I hate myself just the right amount for being so cheesy.

We hadn't, however, let anyone else know about our budding romance. Grim knew, since he and I could speak telepathically, and I wasn't always the best at keeping my personal thoughts from spilling over into my communication with him. And because Grim knew, so did Ruby. The two couldn't communicate directly, but Grim and Ruby's familiar, Clifford, could, and the two grumpy canines spent most of their waking hours—which were, admittedly, few—gossiping like teenagers. It hadn't taken long before Clifford passed along the intel to Ruby, who later claimed she already knew.

She did, after all, have the gift of Insight, like all Fifth Wind witches. Although, it didn't take a magical ability to guess what was going on when Tanner looked at me through those gorgeous hazel eyes. Clearly, no one had ever told him about playing hard to get, keeping his cards close to the vest.

And that was one of the many things I liked about him.

"You'll want to start with the crystals," he said, leading me past one glass case after another, toward the back of the store. The place looked more like a high-end jewelry store than what I'd expected for a wand shop. It was clean, bright, with each model on a delicate stand under thick (and I assumed enchanted) glass.

Brooms floated in midair around the edge of the showroom, bobbing gently like buoys, each one a slight variation of color, shape, and bristle from the next. Could I ride a broom? I was still so unclear on what was and wasn't within my witchy abilities. But more importantly, did I *want* to ride a broom?

I was leaning toward no. I'd seen witches flying around town on those, and it looked so uncomfortable. Some rode sidesaddle, which looked silly and antiquated, while others straddled the broom, which, um, ouch. Seemed like a quick way to get a UTI.

"How do I decide which crystal to get in my wand?" I asked.

"You can get a pretty good sense based on what kind of witch you are. Then from there, it's mostly feeling it out. Sometimes you have to take a few for a test drive. Ezra can also help. He's been doing this for years."

I glanced back toward the counter where he stood chatting with Ruby. "Couldn't be that long. He doesn't look a day older than I am."

"Uh, I think he's in his seventies. But he might be older."

"Come again?" I said. "I thought he was a witch. Don't witches age?" If Ruby were any indication, they did.

When I glanced at Tanner, a momentary panic swept over me. He was a witch and he looked in his late twenties, a few years younger than me, but what if he was three hundred? What if I aged and he didn't?

He did me the favor of squashing that fear, though. "Most do. I'm not entirely sure why Ezra doesn't." Tanner leaned close, a conspiratorial half-grin drawing my attention to those soft lips framed by his day-old dirty-blond stubble. "My guess is that he either performed some dark spell to keep him young, or being surrounded by so many powerful objects all the time has slowed the aging process."

"I hope it's the first," I said. "That's a way better story."

Something ignited in Tanner's eyes, and I knew what was about to happen. But not right here where anyone could see us, right?

He already had a solution in mind, though, and yanked me after him, behind a wall leading toward the back that cut off the visibility from the counter and the front door. Then he pulled me into him, my body pressed against his, my hands on his warm, firm chest, and he kissed me.

"Oh, for fang's sake."

My body tensed, and I cracked open my eyes, already certain of the judgment waiting for me in the form of a giant, black hound with a small munchkin cat on his back.

"Grim," I said, not bothering with telepathy. "Stop being a creep. If you don't like it, you and Monster can go entertain yourselves elsewhere."

"Monster!" Tanner said sharply. His familiar must've been making similar comments to Grim's that I couldn't hear. "You know better."

We shoo-ed away our familiars, but the moment was somewhat lost. "I guess we should get back to shopping," he said.

"It *is* why we're here." I sighed and dropped my hands from his body. "I hate shopping." And I hated it even more when it interfered with the small bits of time outside of work that I could sneak with this beautiful West Wind witch.

We approached Ruby and Ezra, who, if I didn't know any better, were flirting with each other.

Ruby was giggling, color in her face as her fingertips glided back and forth over her collarbone where it peaked out from her dark, loose robes. Ezra winked at her before turning to face Tanner and me, still wearing a contagiously goofy grin. "Ruby tells me you're looking for a necromancer's wand."

I nodded. "You're going to have to walk me through it step-by-step, though, because I don't even know where to start."

"I can do that," he said, "especially for a promising and beautiful young witch such as yourself."

Tanner bristled beside me, but there was no need. Ezra was attractive, with cocoa skin and a troublemaker's grin, but I wasn't a man-hopper.

Sure, I used to be, but that was because the caliber of men I was dealing with was so much lower than Tanner. No, Tanner was his own breed. He had the resilience and strength of a man, and the gentle innocence of a boy. Life had thrown Tanner about as much misfortune as it had me, but he'd managed to keep an openness to him rather than becoming bitter and shut off like, eh-hem, *some* people.

But I was getting better, and being with Tanner was a step in the right direction. I wouldn't just ditch him for the next handsome man who called me beautiful.

"Follow me," said Ezra, coming around the counter. "You'll want to start with crystals."

"I already told her that," Tanner said assertively.

Ezra paused, turned toward us, his eyes flickering between Tanner and me, then he bit his lips and said, "Ah. Right. Good thinking, Tanner."

We followed him to a glass cabinet mounted on the wall, where crystals of all shapes, opacities, and colors gleamed. "You're going to want a protective crystal," he said, "assuming your day-to-day is anything like Ms. True's." He grinned mischievously at Ruby, who giggled again.

Wait a second. Did Ezra and Ruby have a history? There was definitely more to the story, though I was fairly certain I didn't want to hear it.

He slid out a tray with an assortment of crystals resting on velvet, sprigs of herbs sprinkled around the edges. "There are different families of crystals suited for different basic functions. Which type of elemental witch you are determines which family we start with. From everything I've seen with my own eyes and read about at length, Fifth Wind witches are best served by protective crystals. Here." He held out a black, jagged stone. "Hold this in your hand. It's black tourmaline. Pretty standard for protection against harmful energies."

It was cool in my hand and heavier than it looked. I rolled it around a bit, unsure what I was looking for. "It's nice," I said, trying to be polite.

Ezra snatched it away. "Yeah, not quite the level of enthusiasm we're looking for."

"What level *are* you looking for?" I asked. "I'm not super into rocks, so I don't know if—"

"You'll know," he said simply. "Here, try this one. Jet.

It's useful for clearing energy, especially if you're an empath."

I'd hardly felt the weight of it in my hand before Ruby said, "Don't think that's a problem for this one. Feelings aren't really her strong suit."

I shot her a dirty look.

But also, she had a point, and the jet didn't feel like anything special to me.

We went through a few more crystals whose names I couldn't remember, none of them striking me as anything other than a rock. Granted, some were *pretty* rocks. The fluorite and blue kyanite, especially.

Before long, though, I'd held each of the crystals on the velvet tray and none had been right. Ezra appeared perplexed, and he tapped on his lips with his index finger as his eyes searched vaguely around the store. "Huh. Let's give this a shot," he said, leading us over to the other side of the store. "I've never used this for a wand, but I'm always up for a challenge." He opened a glass case with heavy amulets and pulled one out by its chain. "Try this."

When the rough stone hit my palm—maybe even before that—I felt it immediately. It was like I'd had vertigo since arriving in Eastwind four and a half months before but had grown used to the sensation, and now, finally, the world stopped spinning. My feet were planted firmly under me. I felt present. I was on solid ground.

"Yeah," he said, grinning shamelessly. "I had a feeling." He wagged a finger at me. "I *thought* I sensed an open door on you."

"What's he talking about?" Tanner asked me.

"Not entirely sure."

He turned to Ezra. "What're you talking about?"

Ezra's reply wasn't addressed to me or Tanner. Instead, he looked past us to Ruby. "Does she know?"

"Oh, yes," Ruby said, holding up a pink crystal to the light to inspect it. "I've already scolded her about it. Never fear."

"That's staurolite," Ezra explained. "I'm going to take a wild guess and say you've channeled a spirit already."

Whoops.

I looked at Tanner, who hadn't learned that detail about me yet. It didn't seem relevant, honestly. I'd only done it once so that a ghost could say her last goodbye to her husband without me being privy to the marital dirty-talk between them. I'd allowed the spirit of Heather Lovelace to channel through me and use my hand to write her X-rated wifely thoughts to her husband.

Listen, it'd seemed like the thing to do at the time.

It wasn't until later that I realized what I'd actually done, and Ruby had been kind enough to lecture me incessantly about the dangers of channeling before I was trained for it. Had I known the risks, specifically that Heather could have taken possession of my body and made me act out all her weird werewolf fantasies with her husband, duh, I wouldn't have done it. We all make mistakes, right?

Tanner's openmouthed expression was one of awe, fear, concern ... and maybe desire. Or I was just projecting that last one. Who's to say?

"Yes. I channeled. Just once, though. And I didn't really know what I was doing." This was stupid. I shouldn't have to defend myself to Ezra and Tanner. They weren't with me at the Lovelace home when I had to tell a husband that his wife wasn't at peace, but rather, in the room with us, the same wife everyone had told him offed herself rather than the truth: that she was murdered by her psychopathic nix sister-in-law for inheritance money.

"Staurolite is a grounding crystal," Ezra said. "It helps keep you planted in space and time. Sometimes those who can transcend into the spirit realm have a hard time keeping both feet among the living. Can't have you living your life with one foot in the grave." He winked again, and I found it *much* less charming this time.

I stared at the rock in my hand. It looked more like two rusty nails in an X, stuck in a clunk of cement. This store was chock full of beautiful stones, yet *this* was the one that struck a chord with my vibration or whatever? It could have just as easily been a chip off some ancient gravestone.

So, in a way, I supposed it made sense. But it still sucked that I didn't get one of the pretty ones.

"Like I said, I've never put it in a wand—the distinctive cross shape of it makes it difficult to fit without compromising the structural integrity. But I always love trying new things."

Ruby pushed between Tanner and me to get a closer look at the stone. "While remembering the appeal of the older things, too, I assume," she added offhandedly.

Ezra laughed. "You know it, Ruby."

"*Question,*" Grim said, padding up with Monster asleep between his shoulder blades. "*Why does it smell overwhelmingly like pheromones over here?*"

"*Wasn't me,*" I said, glancing from Ezra to Ruby, trying to interpret the strange look passing between them.

"Unfortunately," Ezra said, "I'm running at a bit of a

delay, so you can expect a three-week wait on any custom-made wands."

"Bummer." I extended the staurolite amulet toward him, but he pushed my hand away gently. "I suggest you hold onto that in the meantime, wear it around, see how it feels. It's not terribly expensive, and if you decide you don't want to keep it once your wand is ready, I'll just apply it as credit toward the purchase."

"Deal."

"Follow me and we can pick out your wand's wood next."

Tanner grabbed my arm gently, getting my attention as we followed Ezra. "You didn't tell me you channeled someone."

"I forgot about it, sorry."

He shook his head, obviously not buying that, but he didn't dispute it verbally. "Who was it?"

"Heather," I said.

"Heather Lovelace?" His eyes went wide and his voice rose, making Ruby glance back at us with an arched eyebrow.

"Yes."

"Are you okay?"

I stopped walking and turned to face him, staring into his eyes. I wanted to kiss him—that tended to be my impulse whenever I so much as glimpsed his gorgeous jaw, sculpted Greek nose, and cupid's bow—but opted instead to place a hand on the side of his face and just *think* about kissing him.

It was far less satisfying.

"I'm fine, Tanner. Seriously."

"You tend to jump into things before you know

anything about them, though," he said. "Don't get me wrong, your fearlessness is"—he leaned forward—"super sexy. But it's not a smart way to live around here."

"I hear you. And I'm working on the channeling thing with Ruby. Don't worry."

Tanner had made it clear on more than one occasion that he felt responsible for my survival, not just because we were dating, or whatever was actually going on, but because, and this was one of the most adorable things in the world, he had been my first point of contact after I'd wrecked my car in Texas, died, and woke up to find myself in the middle of the Deadwoods in Eastwind. He took that responsibility seriously, and every time I did something dangerous, he felt like he'd failed in his role.

He never said all these things, of course, but men aren't *that* hard to read, especially when they haven't intentionally spent decades practicing the art of hiding all emotion. Tanner tended to let it all hang out.

Or maybe I *was* slightly empathetic.

Nah. I had intuition, or Insight, as it was called, but Ruby was right. Emotions weren't really my thing. That's why it'd felt so strange when, after channeling Heather, I could still feel some of her residual emotion lingering inside me, even after she'd left this realm and traveled beyond the veil for good. It was like a hangover that took me a full week to shake.

I admit that it's not *ideal* for emotions to feel like a hangover. But we all have our shortcomings.

Once I'd settled on ivy wood for my wand, Ezra scribbled down the specifications in a book, and I paid him for the amulet. It wasn't cheap, but it was actually a relief to unburden myself of some of the wages I didn't know how to spend. In Eastwind, the bare necessities came cheap, and because I didn't have time to drink, had no desire for a shopping spree, and ate most of my meals for free during my shifts at Medium Rare, I didn't know what to do with the piles of coins amassing in the room I rented from Ruby. I hadn't yet struck up the nerve to visit the bank and open an account, not since I heard that the place was run by dragon-shifters. While I was getting used to facing dangerous beasts on a daily basis, dragon-shifters struck me as expert-level stuff. I wasn't ready for it. Maybe once I had my wand handy and felt a little more confident with some defensive spells I could handle it, but not before.

By the time we finished up at Ezra's Magical Outfitters, Grim was already on a tear. *"My stomach is eating itself. I don't think I'm going to make it to Ruby's. Just leave me here to die. Or just bring me some Franco's meatballs. Either way. Your choice. No pressure."*

I wanted to tell Grim to reel it in, but then my stomach growled, and I saw his ears perk up at the sound, so I had no ground to stand on.

"Dinner?" I said as our group stood in the late-June dusk outside on the cobblestone streets.

"Sheehan's Pub isn't far off," Tanner said. "I've been meaning to take you there forever."

My heart plummeted into my empty stomach. Sheehan's Pub.

I'd fetishized this place over the past months. I'd walked by it but had never gone in, and my best guess was that it was just a dumpy, dark pub with greasy fried food that lacked proper seasoning, and all the career drunks Eastwind had to offer.

But in my mind, it was a sort of finish line for Tanner and me. And a starting line.

"Yeah, let's do it," I said like everything was normal and my blood sugar wasn't bottoming out as a result of hunger and adrenaline.

"You two have fun," Ruby said. "Not really my style. I think I'll just stop by the butcher's on the way back and stick with beef stew tonight. You two lovebirds have fun, though."

"Lovebirds?" I said. "We're not—"

"Lock the door when you get back," she said, cutting me off before heading the opposite way from Sheehan's, toward home. Clifford trotted behind her.

"*It's a tough call,*" Grim said. "*On the one hand, I could come watch you two put your hands all over each other, which would likely result in my vomiting pure stomach acid at this point, or I could go with Ruby, sit by the fire, eat beef stew scraps, and not have your pheromones invading my sinuses. Hm. Whatever will I choose?*"

"*I thought you were too famished to walk,*" I replied.

"*Helena the Mighty thought she was too injured to keep fighting the onslaught of the witches at the Battle of Obsidian Summit, but she managed to pull through, given the right incentive.*"

"*Was that incentive beef stew?*"

"*No. It was the head of Miss Mary on a spike.*"

"*And did she get it?*"

"*Uh, no. Helena was mowed down almost immediately. She and the rest of the werewolves were slaughtered in droves in that battle.*"

"*Um.*"

"Okay, so it wasn't the best example. Blame it on my fatigue."

"Monster says she doesn't want to come," Tanner said, interrupting my not-so-enlightening conversation.

"Yeah, Grim is saying the same ... in so many words."

Tanner looked confused. "He's worried about getting eaten by a werebear?"

"Oh. No. He thinks he's going to starve to death."

"They have food there."

"I know." I turned to Grim. "Yeah, get out of here. Go beg from Ruby for all I care."

As Monster rode Grim into the sunset, Tanner and I started toward Sheehan's Pub.

Finally, it was about to happen.

Although I wasn't sure what "it" was.

Chapter Two

"No way!" came a shout from inside Sheehan's as my eyes slowly adjusted to the dim lighting.

Then I spotted Jane heading toward us.

"I can't believe it," she said, shoving Tanner out of the way to get a clear shot at hugging me. "You're actually doing something outside of work." Then she added, "Oh, hi, Tanner."

"He's the one responsible for bringing me," I said, trying to give him some credit.

Jane leaned back slightly, her eyes wide. "Uh-huh. You two came together, then?"

Tanner nodded, but I added, "I mean, we're here at the same time. So, yeah, I guess you could say that."

Pressing her lips together and squinting at me, her voice sounded tight when she said, "Okay then." Then she shot me a we'll-talk-about-this-later look and headed over to a large corner booth where Ansel, Donovan, and a younger blond man I hadn't met before sat, each sipping from large tankards.

Ansel was the warmest toward me as we approached, which wasn't saying much. I didn't suspect that Jane's fiancé disliked me, but it did seem like every time I spoke with him, it was in the context of solving a murder, and while he wasn't always a suspect, it didn't make for the most personal of interactions. Or maybe it made for *too* personal of interactions.

The young blond man stared at me with wide eyes, like maybe I was a threat, while Donovan ...

Well, Donovan offered me the same disdainful look as usual through his piercing blue eyes. It might make me sound shallow to admit it, but having someone as painfully hot as Donovan, with his dark hair, high cheekbones and pouty pink lips, act like he was passing a cactus-shaped kidney stone every time he laid eyes on me didn't feel spectacular.

But then his gaze landed on Tanner, his best friend, and his expression changed completely. His eyes softened around the edges, and those sculpted lips parted to reveal pearly white teeth as he grinned. "Tanner! Can't think of the last time I saw you around here."

I decided to try an experiment. I stopped my progress and let Tanner go ahead of me. My hypothesis proved correct. As soon as I was obscured from the view of the booth's inhabitants and Tanner was fully visible, the mood shifted dramatically, and everyone was grinning and joking around in a heartbeat, giving Tanner grief for his long work hours while clearly glad to have him back.

Huh.

This was something to consider. Specifically, that Tanner was easily the town's most beloved witch, while I'd done an efficient job of making everyone in town associate me with death, murder, and suspicion in just a matter of months. And yet, *I* was the reluctant one to openly admit Tanner and I were together.

It didn't make a whole lot of sense initially, and I decided I would think about it later.

Because for now, I was at a pub, I was starving, and I wanted whatever cool beverage was causing sweat to drip down the sides of the metal tankard Donovan clutched in his hand.

I watched him shut his eyes as he leaned his head back, watched his Adam's apple bob as the cold drink rushed down his throat.

Why couldn't this jerk just like me?

I turned around before I ever made it to the booth and headed straight to the bar.

An auburn-haired dwarf nodded a curt hello as I squeezed next to his barstool.

"Hi," I said.

"Hello."

"I'm Nora."

He nodded, his eyes roaming quickly up and down the top half of me. "That's good to know." He turned his attention toward something behind the bar as I stared at him, unsure what to say to that.

"Nora!" said a sweet sing-song voice.

I followed the dwarf's eyeline and had to stand on my tiptoes before I spotted a head of orange-red hair on the opposite side of the bar. "Oh! Hey, Fiona!"

Fiona Sheehan, a leprechaun who I'd only spoken to once, (and not under the best of circumstances, considering her boyfriend, Bruce Saxon, had just been murdered by his *other* girlfriend, who Fiona didn't know was still in the picture), beamed at me. I wracked my brain for what exactly I'd said in our sole conversation that would make her like me rather than associated me with death, mourning, etc.

Oh, right. I'd lied to her.

I'd told her that Bruce had talked all about her in his brief existence between the planes. The truth, though, was that he'd only mentioned her by mistake. She was his secret girlfriend, and if he hadn't slipped and called his murderess by Fiona's name, I never would have known about her at all.

I didn't realize she worked at Sheehan's Irish Pub, but, um, duh. Her family must own it. It had probably been passed down through generations of Sheehans.

Fiona stood on the other side of the bar and grinned at me with her big, round, childlike eyes. It wasn't hard to see why Bruce Saxon might be a little reckless if it meant dating her. She was gorgeous and had a sweetness to her that seemed, honestly, out of place in such a dank establishment.

"I haven't seen you in here before. Is this your first visit?"

"Yeah," I said, "I'm a little embarrassed to admit that it is."

Her giggle reminded me of a piccolo. "Word around town is that you're a busy woman. Working long hours at Medium Rare *and* solving the murders Deputy Manchester can't handle." Her smiled faded slightly at the mention of murders. "What can I get you? Drinks and food on me tonight."

"Why?" I didn't mean for it to come shooting out of my mouth, but can you blame me for being shocked after the less than warm reception from Donovan, Ansel, and whoever that blond man-boy was?

"Nora!" she said, surprised herself. "Because you put Bruce's murderer behind bars!" She leaned forward, so I did, too. "You know what he meant to me."

"Right." I looked around, curious who might've overheard. While no one seemed to be paying any attention, I did recognize a few more familiar faces among the full house. At a high-top in the corner, Lucent Lovelace regaled a fiery-haired leprechaun with some story or another that involved Lucent banging his fist on the table repeatedly while his audience of one howled with laughter. Where the bar turned at a ninety-degree angle sat a figure all dressed in black, his sickle leaning against the bar. And on the stool next to Ted, Eastwind's grim reaper, sat a dashing, well-dressed man in perhaps his late thirties, who sipped red wine gracefully.

Between the grim reaper and this stranger stood a young pretty woman who, if one didn't know Ted personally, one might assume was in mortal danger.

Zoe Clementine spotted me and waved me over, and a second later, Ted and the stranger looked my direction.

I returned my attention to Fiona momentarily. "I could go for something fried and heavily seasoned to eat, and whatever drink you prefer, please. I better go say hi." I nodded over at the threesome, and Fiona agreed with a chipper nod.

"Nora!" Ted said as soon as I approached. He was much friendlier than one might expect a grim reaper to be, but his voice—a deep death rattle like dry bones skittering over a chalkboard—matched his morbid appearance just fine. "I never thought I'd see you out and about in Eastwind." He chuckled and it sent shivers down my spine and out to my fingertips. "Figured I'd have to go to Medium Rare forever just to get my fix."

Yikes. A little bit of flirting at a pub was to be expected, but Ted's attentions weren't limited to the pub. They followed me all the way to my job, much like the overwhelming sense of my own mortality followed me whenever Ted was near.

"Tanner convinced me to come out," I said.

"Ah." His shrouded head drooped. "Makes sense."

"Are you and Tanner Culpepper together?" asked the well-dressed man I didn't recognize.

I blinked a few times at his forwardness, and he flashed me a cocky grin before extending his hand. "We haven't met. Sebastian Malavic." Eastwind had a lot of strange accents, but Sebastian's was distinct with flourishes of Eastern European woven into his vowels.

I'd heard the name. Everyone in Eastwind had. He wasn't just Sebastian Malavic, he was *Count* Sebastian Malavic. He held a seat on the High Council as Eastwind's treasurer, the theory being that someone as rich as him would have no interest in pilfering from the measly Eastwind funds. I happened to think that was a stupid theory based on the weak assumption that he hadn't amassed his wealth from that exact activity over a long period of time.

And as I shook his hand and felt the coldness of his skin on mine, I remembered another detail about Sebastian: he was a vampire. One of the oldest, if the gossip was correct. "Nora Ashcroft," I said, meeting his eyes.

I made a point of meeting the eyes of men like this.

You know, the ones who have been in power so long they forget they even have it. Yet they're the first to exercise that power in brash ways and also the first to play victim whenever an ounce of it is distributed to the less fortunate. If you exhibited power or abilities men like this didn't possess and showed any sign of weakness, they would delight in crushing you.

Yes, I got all this from our short interaction. I have Insight, after all. But even if I didn't, I'd met plenty of men like Sebastian before.

Along with meeting his eyes, I went in for the kill with the handshake, squeezing as hard as I could without showing signs of strain. And then I saw it. It was almost imperceptible. It was a small flicker around his eyes—I'd surprised him. And he liked it. Men like this also enjoyed surprises; wielding so much power could be boring for them. I wasn't here to be his challenge, his prey to overpower, though.

"Isn't she just great?" Zoe said, her shoulders bouncing like a buoy in choppy waters. "Have you ever met anyone like her?"

"No," Sebastian said simply, staring straight at me. When he turned his gaze to Zoe and a splinter of smile crept onto his face as his eyes roamed up and down her body, I had an instant desire to pull her out of there away from the vampire and let her know in no uncertain terms what was going on. He had his eye on her. He'd singled her out as a target, though for what and why, I wasn't sure.

"It's such a crazy coincidence that just a few weeks after Ruby True retires, we get a brand new Fifth Wind into Eastwind, isn't it?" Zoe remarked breathlessly.

"I don't believe in coincidences," Sebastian spat.

Psh. Of course he didn't. He probably thought everything that happened in Eastwind was an aftershock of some action he'd taken. The unfortunate midair broom collision that made *The Eastwind Watch* the other day? Probably a result of him doing a few extra push-ups in his strict morning routine.

"I'm so excited you're here, Nora!" Zoe said in her usual bubbly way. She was always excited people were anywhere. I could bump into her as we fled a deranged werewolf pack in the Deadwoods, and she'd still say she was excited I was there. But at the same time, I had a weakness for naiveté. I didn't understand it, but I admired it. Case in point: Tanner.

"You're always working," Zoe continued, "so I figured you didn't want to go out and about. Otherwise I totally would've invited you to hang—"

"You never answered my question," Sebastian said, interrupting her.

I jerked my head around to glare at him, but managed at the last second to keep my hand by my side rather than smacking him for his rudeness.

"Which was?" I asked, keeping my voice casual.

"Are you and the Culpepper boy together?"

I forced a sweet smile. "Well, he's not a boy, first of all, and to answer your question, Tanner and I co-own Medium Rare, so what do you think? Would dating be a smart idea?"

He grinned. "No, but it could be terribly exciting. Think of all the possible complications. You'd have to hide it from others to keep things professional and avoid employees claiming you received preferential treatment, of course. Sounds quite arousing, if you ask me."

Yeah, I wasn't huge on Sebastian. That was an easy conclusion to draw. He acted like he knew me. And the worst part about it? He kind of did. While I was sizing him up to a tee, he was doing the same to me.

Not cool.

I grinned. "Whatever you say, Stefan." I let him suck on the wrong name for a while. God knows it drove me nuts when people messed up mine. Then I excused myself, making a special effort to give a warm parting to both Zoe and Ted (my rebuke of Sebastian appeared to leave him in better spirits than the mention of Tanner had), and went back to the booth where my boss, business partner, and maybe soon-to-be-boyfriend was sitting with the rest of the group.

Jane had squeezed in next to Ansel, and when I approached, Tanner jumped up, letting me slide in.

Right next to Donovan.

Oof. I did not want to be the filling of a Tanner and Donovan sandwich.

Or maybe ...

I glanced at Donovan who ignored me purposefully.

Okay, nope. Impractical fantasy averted.

"Nora, this is Landon Hawker," Tanner said, and as I shook the blond's hand, Tanner explained, "He works down in the Parchment Catacombs."

"Nice to meet you," I said.

He stared at me through his thick-rimmed glasses, and I wasn't sure if his cheeks were always that flushed or if whatever he was drinking had brought out the color. "Nora Ashcroft? Really?" he said.

"Yep. Last I checked."

"Huh."

"What?"

"Nothing, nothing."

I leaned in front of Donovan, ignoring his exasperation, to hear Landon better. "No, what is it? Come on." I touched his arm gently. "Is it the Fifth Wind witch thing? Does it freak you out?"

His eyes shot wide. "What? No! Not at all! I think it's cool, actually."

"Well, that makes one of us." I leaned back as Fiona brought over a plate of steaming fried chicken with dipping sauce and a metal tankard, setting them in front of me.

"What'd you get?" Tanner asked excitedly, rubbing his hands together.

"Not exactly sure. But I'm ready to find out."

Fiona winked. "Let me know when you're ready for your next round, Nora."

As she walked away, Tanner reached for my plate and I slapped his hand away. "Nuh-uh. This ain't a dang commune. Go get your own." He laughed, slid out of the booth and chased after Fiona, leaving me in unnecessary proximity to Donovan. I scooted over.

Nibbling off the tip of a chicken strip, I said, "So, you're a ... witch? Is that rude to ask?"

"No, not rude" he said, pushing his glasses further up the bridge of his nose. "And yes. A North Wind witch."

Slowly but surely, I was getting better at this bizarre guessing game. "Ooh, an aeromancer."

He cringed slightly. "We don't use that word anymore."

25

"Huh? Why not?"

"It's a little outdated."

"Does that mean I shouldn't go around calling myself a necromancer?"

He swallowed hard, but before he could respond, Donovan jumped in. "If you want everyone to avoid you, you should definitely keep using that term."

I feigned shock. "Wait, you mean I could get you to avoid me *more* by just calling myself a necromancer?"

"It's not right," Landon said, "but necromancy still freaks people out. They don't understand it, I think. They haven't had enough exposure to it."

"And you have?" Donovan said.

Landon shrugged. "I've read all about it. And, I mean, look at her. Does she seem like the kind of person to awaken an evil spirit?"

Landon was all right in my book.

I struggled to keep a straight face as Donovan looked at me, apparently assessing whether I was the type to turn an army of demons against Eastwind.

... Wow, he was giving it just a little too much thought. This should be a no-brainer.

Finally he said, "No. Not intentionally at least. But I've heard enough to know she can get herself into trouble just fine."

"Oh please, you think I'd accidentally raise an army of demons against the town?"

He jerked his head back. "Huh? I didn't say anything about an army of demons."

"What? No. Me neither." I quickly sipped my drink, enjoying the rich bitterness of a porter as it washed over my taste buds.

"Nora," said Jane, finally breaking from her intimate conversation with Ansel. "Since you're on the market, Ansel and I think you should meet his best friend Darius."

"Yeah," Ansel said, "I think you two might hit it off. He doesn't take no unicorn swirls from anyone either."

I could feel Donovan's cool blue gaze boring into the side of my face. "Not really looking. Thanks, though."

Jane and Ansel shared a satisfied glance, and Ansel nodded slightly. I swore I heard him say, "You called it, sugarpaws."

Tanner reappeared, and just before he slid in beside me, I stopped him. "Restroom?"

He pointed to a dark hallway at the back corner of the pub.

Oh, lovely. "Thanks." I scooted by him and made for it.

The bathrooms were at the very end of a bend, and I didn't feel entirely safe, but the porter had taken the edge off my anxiety and added just enough liquid to the tank that I pushed on.

As I stepped out of the ladies room, I jumped when I nearly bumped right into someone.

"Geez, Tanner. You scared the—"

He pressed me up against the wall and kissed me. Then he broke the kiss and stared down at me. "Sorry. It's just too hard to be around you and have to pretend we're not together. It's killing me."

I pushed him away gently. "Stop it. You're fine."

"Why can't we just be honest with people about it?"

"You know why. We've been over this."

He crinkled his nose and pinched his eyes shut as he

shook his head. "Jane won't care. And I doubt Greta, Anton, or Bryant will care as long as you don't get preferential treatment. Which you won't." He grinned and pressed me to the wall again. "Not at work, at least."

I sighed. He made solid points. But still, something held me back. Maybe Sebastian was right. Maybe I enjoyed the excitement of secrecy.

No. Sebastian couldn't be right.

To stop my brain, I kissed Tanner again.

Then suddenly, "Oh, for fang's sake." I broke the kiss and jerked my head around to see Donovan glaring at us.

"It's not—" Tanner began.

"You said nothing was happening between you two." Donovan made no effort to hide his disdain, but he raised his hands in surrender. "It's fine. Who you mess around with is your business. I just think you can do a lot better."

"Huh?" Tanner said, but Donovan had already disappeared into the men's room.

Tanner made to go after him, but I grabbed his arm. "Stop. It doesn't matter. Do you think he'll tell anyone else?"

"No. Donovan's not a gossip. What he said, Nora. It's not true."

"Don't worry about it. I know he's not my biggest fan." I tried to force a smile to the surface, but I'm fairly sure it came out as a weird cringe. "I'd better go out ahead of you, or else, you know."

"Sure."

I'd only just made it out of the dark hallway and into the slightly less dark bar, which now seemed sunny by comparison, when I felt a strong hand wrap around my wrist.

I whirled around and was face-to-face with Lucent Lovelace. "Nora. I thought that was you when you walked by."

Twisting my wrist free of his grasp, I said, "Hi Lucent. How's it going?"

"Oh, you know. Love of my life is still dead, and all I have is her money and a big empty house to keep me company. Oh, and whiskey." He raised his glass. "Lots of whiskey."

"I can smell," I said.

"You haven't introduced me, you idiot," said the leprechaun across the table from Lucent. "You trying to keep her all for yourself, eh?"

"Nope," I said quickly.

"Seamus Shaw," he said, "pleased to make your acquaintance, but would also be pleased to get to know you more intimately."

"Ew." Not the response he was expecting, though it truly should've been. He was slobbering drunk, which was surprising, given how he appeared to be sweating out the booze faster than anyone could reasonably take it in. Seamus's name often came up in conversations around town, and never in a positive light. Now, I could see why.

"You say that, but before long I'll have you saying, 'Oh! Ohh!' That's a guarantee."

Before I could tell him I wasn't into short guys, Tanner appeared out of nowhere. "I think you need to go home, Seamus," he said sternly, stepping between the leprechaun and me.

"Tanner," I said, "it's fine."

"No, it's not." His eyes remained on Seamus. "You don't get to speak to her that way. You're drunk and being inappropriate. You need to leave." He turned to Lucent. "Get him out of here. Now."

"Who do you think you are?" Seamus said, but Lucent nodded, grabbing his drinking buddy by the arm, and dragging him out.

The agitation from Seamus's disgusting comments might have leaked through just a little when I rounded on Tanner. "I can take care of myself," I hissed. "I don't need a knight in shining armor."

His shocked confusion stirred immediate guilt inside me, though I wasn't sure if it was because he thought I would appreciate the gesture, or because he didn't know what a knight in shining armor was.

"I know you can handle yourself," he said blankly.

I bit my lips, deciding not to respond. And then my eyes landed on Donovan at the edge of the dark hallway to the bathrooms. He watched the interaction like a hawk, no doubt wondering if he would get to enjoy the entertainment of Tanner and me crashing and burning before we ever truly got off the ground.

I wouldn't give him the satisfaction. "I'm sorry, Tanner. I didn't mean to snap. Thanks. Seamus was being a total creep."

"Yeah, he was," Tanner said, and while he seemed less shocked, the confusion was still there. He put his back to the rest of the pub, then asked. "Are we good?"

I nodded. "Great. But my chicken is getting cold, so we should ..."

"Right! I have some coming, too."

I played my cards just right so that Tanner was next to Donovan in the circular booth and I had the outside. Things went much more smoothly after that, especially once Landon suggested we play a few rounds of Explode a Toad. Don't worry, no animals were harmed in the process. I'd wondered about that, too. But it was just a drinking game like the ones I'd played at parties back in high school. Only, the playing cards were enchanted to disappear and reappear in another person's hand, and the loser had to chug their drink with a tiny conjured toad at the bottom, which, they explained to me only once it was my turn to chug, would disappear again as soon as it reached my stomach and was not in fact a real animal.

Tell that to my esophagus, though.

It was not my favorite game, but it was good for a few laughs, and as the booze kept coming and Ansel lost three games in a row, even Donovan had lightened up and seemed to be enjoying himself.

It wasn't the dream trip to Sheehan's Pub that I'd always imagined, but, in the end, when Tanner walked me home and kissed me one last time on Ruby's porch, it was as good of a visit as I could've asked for.

Chapter Three

I remembered why I didn't bother with a social life as soon as I dragged my butt into Medium Rare the next day. I hadn't drank that much, but because I rarely indulged anymore, the hangover was rearing its ugly head just enough that the bright, magicked interior lights made my eyes roll slightly back into my skull the moment I stepped in from the soothing of pre-dawn darkness outside.

Tanner seemed slightly worse for the wear, too, and greeted me with a lethargic, "Hey, Nora," as he counted out coins at one of the back booths, his head braced on a fist, smooshing half his face upward.

At least I wasn't alone. Because the only thing worse than a hangover is having one when your drinking buddy doesn't.

The lingering dry hum in my head caused me to spend most of the morning fixated on how old I was getting, but that lessened somewhat a few hours later when Ted walked through the door. Was my sense of mortality heightened? Of course. But at least I wasn't as ancient as Ted. Did he have an age, or was he as old as time? Or, I guess, as old as life? Because time can exist without life, but life can't exist without death, right?

Oh, geez. I was getting philosophical again. That was one of my weird side effects of being hungover, like my mind was withdrawing inward to ignore all the negative physical sensations.

Grim, who had entered only a half hour earlier after getting his necessary sixteen hours of sleep, stirred awake when I stepped over him to grab the coffee pot from its cradle at the corner of the countertop. I went ahead and poured myself a third cup of coffee before dishing some up for Ted, who made a pit stop by the counter before heading to his usual spot in the corner.

"How you feeling this morning?" he asked cheerfully as I set the mug down in front of him.

"Fantastic. You're not here for me, are you? Because my head feels like maybe you are."

He sat up straight. "Huh? No, I'm just here for the usual. I started coming here long before you were ever in Eastwind. Heh."

Wow. Not what I meant. "No, I just mean, I feel like I'm going to die." I waved it off. "I'm just being melodramatic. Sorry. Bad joke."

"Right. No. I got that. Also, need I repeat that I don't 'come for people' per se? I just clean up after them. I am in no way a death omen."

"So brag about it," Grim moaned from the floor by my feet.

"I know, Ted. Don't worry." I forced a grin to satisfy him. "I'm just teasing you. You know, like friends do."

33

His hood fell back slightly, revealing the jagged bones of his nose. "Friends? Right. Friends. We're friends." He grabbed the coffee and cheers-ed me with it. "Here's to you feeling better, friend, so that I don't have to clean up your corpse! Heh."

"Well, that's unsettling," Grim said, as Ted marched over to his corner booth.

I glanced down at him. *"Which part?"*

"Take your pick."

As the groggy early morning customers cleared out or became more functionally caffeinated, the gossip began to flow faster than the coffee.

"Nora," said Hyacinth Bouquet as I passed her table. I stopped in my tracks. "More coffee?"

"Huh? Oh, sure. But I was just going to say that I heard about last night. At Sheehan's."

My mind flashed back to the look of disdain on Donovan's face when he caught Tanner and me kissing by the bathrooms. "What about it?" I held my breath.

"Seamus, that dumb screw-up. He was making lewd comments, and then Tanner stepped in and put him in his place." She sighed and turned to her husband, who was reading *The Eastwind Watch* and, in my opinion, was giving off fairly clear signals that he did not want to be dragged into the gossip. "Isn't Tanner just the sweetest boy, James?"

James grunted, which was more than I'd expected from him. Hyacinth turned back to me, placing a hand on my arm. "Oh, Nora, you're lucky he was there to stand up for you, but really, you shouldn't be going to a place like that. As I've told you before, you'd be a hit at Lyre Lounge. And I think I remember something about

Seamus being banned from there a while back, so you wouldn't have to worry about him. Much better company at Lyre. And richer." She waggled her eyebrows at me. "You wouldn't have to work here anymore, if you found yourself a man at Lyre."

"Thanks, but I'm fine, and I enjoyed Sheehan's." I topped up her coffee with a smile and walked away before I said anything I regretted.

My temper was still sizzling like a hot griddle from the interaction when two teen boys I'd only seen a couple times before entered like a hurricane—loud, obnoxious, full of themselves. They strolled in like they owned the place, and I cringed to think about who they would be in five or ten years when they were considered adults.

But then I reminded myself that *most* teen boys were like this and they didn't all turn out to be like Count Sebastian Malavic.

Also, these boys weren't vampires. I wasn't sure what they were, but I was certain they were living, breathing manboys.

I looked around for Tanner, hoping he would pick up the table—after all, he would probably hit it off great with the kids because he usually did—but he was nowhere to be seen. I thought about distracting myself with something else and hoping he would emerge from the back in the meantime, but then I realized I was just being silly and a little bit lazy.

Would these boys tip? Not a chance. But it wasn't like I needed the money. And as owner of this place, I shouldn't be trying to shirk my basic responsibilities.

"Hello, gentlemen. How are you doing today?"

The two boys glanced at each other across the table,

and a devious look passed between them. "Much better, now that you're here," said one with strawberry blond hair, and a round, freckly face punctuated by a pug nose.

The other boy, who had pitch-black hair and was probably a much bigger hit among the teen girls of Eastwind, snickered at his buddy's weak come-on.

I decided to ignore it. "My name's Nora, and I'll be helping you today. What can I get you started to drink? Coffee, orange juice?"

"Not thirsty anymore," said the blond. "I already have a tall drink of water right here." He motioned to me from head to toe, and I arched an eyebrow at him, cocking my head to the side.

"Nice one," I said dryly. "I'm sure that works well on the tweens. Now do you want something to drink, or are you just going to sit here occupying a booth forever so that I can't make a decent tip off it?"

The dark-haired boy cackled, and the blond's face turned pink. "You want a tip? Here's one. You're prettier when you don't speak."

My mouth fell open, but I snapped it shut. I wouldn't let him get to me. I turned to his friend. "How about you? Coffee? OJ?"

"Coffee please, ma'am," he said, smirking.

That was more like it. "Great. I'll be right out with it."

When I turned to walk away, though, is when it happened, and I was pushed right over the edge.

Two fingers and a thumb—I could feel each one distinctly—grabbed the back of my pants, pinching my butt.

I gasped and whirled around, expecting it to be the

blond, but the blond, for all his many apparent faults, redeemed himself slightly by looking absolutely horrorstricken as he stared at his raven-haired friend.

"Get out." I could hardly speak without yelling.

"You can't kick us out," said the offender. I wanted to knock the smug look right off his face, but I, being an adult and the bigger person, miraculously refrained.

"I absolutely can," I said. "In fact, I'm doing it right now."

Okay, yes, I was looking forward to this part. When I owned Chez Coeur back in Austin, kicking out inappropriate customers was often the highlight of my week. So, as off-balance as the pinch had left me, I had my feet under me now. I knew how to do this part.

And I *loved* it.

I stepped back from the booth, allowing them just enough room to squeeze by. I knew they were just kids— dumb ones, yet kids, nonetheless— but if they were going to try to make me feel uncomfortable, I was going to do it right back. They had to learn sometime, and too many women felt unsafe standing up for themselves.

It was my moral responsibility to humiliate these kids, is what I'm saying.

At least, that was my line of reasoning while I was mildly hungover, irked at Hyacinth, and could still feel the spot on my left butt cheek stinging.

The boys didn't move. My best guess was that they were scared stiff. Perfect.

"Did you not hear me?" I said, raising my voice. "I'll say it louder this time, so maybe you hear me. Sexual harassment does *not* fly with me. Now you two little punks need to leave before I *make* you leave."

Not gonna lie. I took quite a bit of satisfaction from it when the restaurant went quiet and all eyes became glued to the two kids who, minutes before, had entered in such a raucous way that they clearly wanted all eyes on them. Be careful what you wish for, I thought.

"You can't kick us out," said the dark-haired one, doubling down like a real idiot. "I want to speak to your manager."

I chuckled. "Yeah, fine." I turned my back on them for just a moment before I spotted Tanner and waved him over, hollering, "Got a second? This boy who grabbed my backside wants to complain about me to you."

Tanner's face broke into a grin. "I dunno. I think they should talk to the owner about that."

I nodded. "Ah yes, good call."

"Fine," said the cocky dark-haired kid. "I want to speak with the owner."

"Certainly," I said. "Oh Nora!" I called over my shoulder, and his face twisted with confusion before I added, "Oh wait. That's me." Then I leaned close and said quietly but firmly. "Get. Out."

This time, both the kids hauled out of there, and didn't look back. The tinkle of the bell above the front door announced the conclusion of the drama, and I breathed a small sigh of relief.

I can't be certain, but I think it was James Bouquet who started applauding first. The rest of the diner followed suit almost immediately.

Tanner appeared beside me. "You were absolutely right, Nora, you don't need me to stand up to men for you."

"They were hardly men."

"Still," he said. "Sorry that my desire to help you with Seamus last night made you think I doubted your ability to take care of yourself. I don't. At all. It's one of the things I like about you, really."

Sheesh. Tanner was like a foreign entity I might never understand. For a second I tried to imagine those words coming out of the mouth of any of the other men I'd dated, and it seemed laughable. "Don't worry about it," I said. "I can take care of myself, but that doesn't mean I don't appreciate a little help every now and then."

He nodded and patted me firmly on the shoulder, maintaining the "friends" act before leaning close and whispering, "I'll help you any which way you want, Nora," then striding away to clear an empty booth.

Tanner's perfection would be the death of me.

At least I knew Ted was around to clean up my corpse whenever that day came to pass.

Chapter Four

"Definitely not your best performance today," Ruby said, as she put a kettle of water on the stove and began scooping out herbs for tea.

"It's been a long day," I replied. The hangover from the night before had cleared up by the end of my shift, but I still felt like I'd run a marathon. My back and feet were killing me, and my brain was sluggish. I'd had little left to give when it came time for my evening lessons.

"That's what happens when you stay out too late with your boyfriend."

Grabbing the stack of rune stones we'd practiced with on the parlor table, I placed them back in their box. "He's not my boyfriend."

"Then you've made an egregious error somewhere along the way."

A tall cabinet by the front door housed most of Ruby's magical tools, and I set the box in its assigned spot. The exact location on the shelf wasn't difficult to find since it was the only space devoid of dust. Ruby hadn't employed much of these tools before I'd tumbled death-first into Eastwind, that much was clear. Magic seemed to work like that here, though. People only needed tools at first. They were like training wheels or the bumpers in a bowling alley. Some people used them forever because it was easier that way, but the really powerful ones stopped bothering with them at a certain point. While Ruby wasn't the kind to show off, I suspected she was much more powerful than she let on. Yet she was the only witch in Eastwind I'd met who was more reluctant to use their magic than Tanner.

"You think being cautious is wrong?"

"There's a difference between caution and avoidance, dear. I'm cautious when I taste my stew for the first time. It could be too hot, or maybe I added too much rosemary. Or maybe the meat is undercooked. But once I get that first taste and realize it's ready and waiting to be eaten, you think I just sit around staring at it? No. You've tasted the broth with that poor, lovesick boy. He's just right. I've known him since he was just a kid, back before those witches did away with his parents—"

"Wait, what?"

"And I can tell you, he's as good as they get. Honestly, I think you're being a little bit stupid. You think some other girl isn't going to come snatch him up the moment she can?"

"Yeah, yeah," I said, "you probably have a point. But go back to that bit about Tanner's parents. I knew they were dead, but I'd never heard—"

A *knock, knock, knock* on the front door caught my attention, but only halfway, since my mind was still lingering on the new information about Tanner.

I grabbed the handle, and before Ruby's shout of "For fang's sake! Don't answer that!" could register with me, I pulled open the door.

The blast of cold whooshed by me and through me, and I only just managed to stay on my feet. It screeched through the downstairs, causing Grim and Clifford to jump up from their spot by the fireplace. Grim tucked his tail between his legs to shield his sensitive bits as his ears laid back flat against his head.

I held my hands over my ears as the wind began to scream like an overheating tea kettle. But as loud as it was, it didn't manage to drown out Ruby as she screamed. "Oh no, you don't! Not in my house!" She closed her eyes and held her hands a foot apart, palms facing each other as she began chanting in a tongue I'd never heard.

The wind whipped around her, coming dangerously close to flipping her robes up over her head and giving me an eyeful of no-thanks.

She ceased her chanting and clapped her hands together three times, and the dry, freezing wind whipped past me again, nearly knocking me over. It flowed faster and faster past me until suddenly it was gone, and the front door slammed shut behind it so hard, I thought it might fall off its hinges. The contents of the cabinet against the front wall rattled on their shelves, marking the departure of whatever I'd just allowed inside.

"That's unfortunate," said Grim.

"You know what that was?"

"No, but I'd put money on this being the beginning of the end for us all. What's that, Cliff? Yeah, good point."

"What'd he say?"

"He said every moment of our lives is the beginning of the end."

I glanced at Clifford as he flopped down again and placed his big, red head on his paws.

"Do you really insist on learning everything the hard way?" Ruby said, straightening her frazzled hair.

"Sorry," I said. "I didn't think about it. What was that?"

She ran her hands down her tangled robes. "Not entirely sure. Probably a demon."

"A *demon*?"

She glared at me, unable to hide her frustration. "Well, *yes*, Nora. What else do you think knocks thrice? We've been over this."

"We haven't been over it being a demon! I didn't even know those were real."

"Of course they are. Not like heaven and hell, biblical kind of demon, but an evil entity, yes. And you just let it in."

"What does that mean?"

She chuckled dryly and turned to the counter where tea leaves and herbs had been blown in every direction. She grunted. "We'll have to wait and see. Likely be another case of caution, not avoidance. Maybe it'll be good practice. Would've preferred we iron out the wrinkles of your love-life in some less threatening way, but life has never been kind to me, so I don't know why it would start now." She peeked in the tea kettle and cursed. "The water's gone. That thing drank all the water!" Turning to me, her eyes shut, she inhaled deeply before saying, "Okay, not to put you into a panic, but if you don't clean up the mess you just made, we're going to have a real problem, you and me."

I backed away slowly toward the staircase. Ruby without her tea did seem like more of a threat to my life than any unnamed evil entity. "Got it," I said. "I'll start on it first thing tomorrow. Promise."

Then I sprinted up the stairs and into my room. I needed a good night sleep if I was going to tackle a mystery like this with so many unknowns.

* * *

As I set out for work in the pre-dawn darkness the next morning, there was still a good portion of me that hoped the incident the night before had been a dream.

I knew better, though.

So instead, I held out hope that it was just a fluke, a one-time thing that didn't actually require any further attention. Problem solved because there was no problem. Sometimes evil entities just dropped by on their way somewhere else, right? Maybe it got the wrong house, realized that, and skedaddled back to the spirit realm, on its merry way.

But then I opened the front door and saw Ruby's garden, and any notion of a best-case scenario flew away like an owl feather on the breeze.

The minimal light from the streetlamp was enough to show me that there would be hell to pay once Ruby woke up.

Her robust herb garden just beyond the porch of her attached townhouse, the same garden that she tended daily with painstaking detail and affection, was completely shriveled. Yes, it was the end of June, and it wasn't exactly ideal weather for most plants, but just the day before, her rosemary bushes had been just fine. So had her sage, and her wormwood, and all the rest.

But now? Nope.

Was it a coincidence? If only.

I considered my options, and *wake up Ruby to tell her that her garden is dead* did not come out on top. So I hurried down the street toward Medium Rare, knowing that whenever I returned, I would have this lovely conversation awaiting me.

However, things took an additional turn for the peculiar on my walk from Ruby's house to Medium Rare. It hadn't just been Ruby's garden that had a hard night. The greenery on either side of the street was in a similar withered state. Because we lived so close to downtown, plant-life wasn't particularly abundant among the stone and wood houses that towered over the streets, just a few shrubs here and there, some patches of grass—no tall trees and only a handful of gardens. But it was clear that nothing along my route had gotten off easy.

Then I passed a cross street and paused when my eyes caught sight of a hanging garden off a balcony that was healthy and flourishing. Why hadn't it been affected like the rest?

My curiosity led the way and I approached the garden, looking for any signs of the same damage done to the other plants.

Nothing.

In fact, none of the plants on this street had been touched.

I walked back toward my route, but continued past

the cross street, checking in the other direction, and it seemed those plants had been spared, too.

After a few more deviations from my route to work, there was only one conclusion I could draw: whatever had shriveled these plants had only functioned on a strict path.

And one that led from Ruby's house to ... where, exactly?

That small mystery was solved shortly, though, when, still following the path of dead plants, I reached Medium Rare and realized that the destruction didn't end. It carried on just a little further ... into the Deadwoods.

Oh boy. While it made sense, it was not a good sign.

And it was where my investigation stopped for the time being. The Deadwoods were nowhere I wanted to be in the full daylight, let alone the earliest light of dawn. The only time I'd ever set foot in there was by accident when I first arrived in Eastwind, where I was woken up by Grim's wet kisses on my face. While it was Grim's home for most of his life and now served as his favorite vacation spot, I wasn't exactly looking for an excuse to step foot in there.

Besides, I had to work. And if I could use that as an excuse, I would.

Trouble had an admirable patience, and I was sure it would still be waiting for me after my shift.

Chapter Five

Mrs. and Mr. Flannery came in as soon as they'd dropped off their pups at Eastwind Primary School for the day. They were in especially high spirits, which was always nice; they could be a little unpredictable. I didn't think it was just because they were werewolves—after all, I knew plenty of werewolves who kept an even keel—but many other Eastwinders chalked it up to that. Seemed a little unfair since everyone should be allowed to have days when they feel chatty and days when they want to be left the heck alone.

"The strangest thing, Nora, did you hear?" Mrs. Flannery said, as I set down two rare steaks with eggs over-easy in front of them.

"Depends on what it is."

"Tammy May's plants just up and died last night."

I tried not to let the sudden tension in my jaw show. "Tammy May?"

"Yes, the fairy who lives over on Obsidian Lane. The one with the cherry tree outside."

Oh yes, I remembered the dead cherry tree on my way to work. "What happened?" I asked.

Mr. Flannery laughed. "Dragon-shifter. I'd put my money on it. The thing looked toasted."

"It did not," Mrs. Flannery scolded. "It wasn't scorched, it was just withered." She leaned toward me. "Kensington just likes to start drama between neighbors." She glared at her husband. "Anywho, I also spoke with Donovan Stringfellow this morning—you know him?"

"Yep."

"And he said Blanche Bridgewater's plants suffered the same fate. You could probably glimpse them after your shift, if you want. The Bridgewater estate isn't terribly far from here."

"I don't like to gawk," I said.

"Nora, dear," Mrs. Flannery said, laughing, "you really should get over that aversion. Gawking is some of the only fun you're allowed to have in this town nowadays, what with the High Council regulating everything magical until we might as well not have magic at all."

"No politics before breakfast, Ginger," said Mr. Flannery.

"True, true." But then she leaned forward conspiratorially. "You know who I think is responsible?"

I swallowed hard. "Who?"

"Ted."

I laughed. "No way. Why would Ted start killing plants?"

"Does he need a reason? He's the town's reaper."

"First of all," I said, trying not to become too annoyed on Ted's behalf, "he doesn't cause the death of anything.

He cleans up after death. He's corrected me on this more than once. It's more a custodial position than anything. Also, why would he suddenly start killing people's plants? He has no motive that I'm aware of."

Mrs. Flannery bit back a smile and sat up straight in her booth, sharing an amused look with her husband. "Look at you, Nora. Always the detective. Looking for motive." She brushed her hand down my arm. "Aren't you just charming? We just adore you, don't we, Kensington?"

Kensington nodded obligingly, but his eyes remained on his steak growing colder by the second while the conversation continued.

So, I excused myself, allowing Mr. Flannery to dig in, and made my way back behind the counter to set down the tray and start a fresh pot in one of the coffeemakers.

Only a moment later, Grim wandered in with Ted holding the door open for him.

Bummer.

Seeing Grim struggle with the front door each morning was a simple joy of mine. Sometimes he even tried to act busy, scratching behind his ear with his hind leg or sniffing the potted plants, until someone else arrived to open the door, then he'd push his way past.

"Morning, Nora!" Ted called.

I poured him a cup of coffee. "Morning, Ted. How's it going?"

"Fantastic! Work's been slow, so I've had plenty of time to explore my new passion."

I indulged him. "Which is?"

"Building fireproof bird houses."

"Oh? Lots of flammable birds out by your place?"

Ted lived in the Deadwoods, which stretched on for miles, so it was only kind of a joke. For all I knew, there were flaming birds shrieking all over the place in there.

"Ha-ha! Nope. But I figure I can sell them at the market. Did you know that over a hundred years ago, the phoenix population in Eastwind was over five thousand? There were flocks of them! Beautiful things. Granted, every now and then they would accidentally set a roof on fire when one of them bit the dust, so, in a way, I understand why people would hunt them in droves, but my hope is that if I can create enough safe habitats for them, they might return."

That was the sweetest and dumbest thing I'd heard all day. But more importantly, it was confirmation that standing up for Ted had been the right thing to do. He would never target random Eastwinders' gardens. "Wow, good for you, Ted. I hope it works out."

"Me too. Knock on wood." He knocked three times, and before my brain could catch up with my reflexes, I grabbed his wrist, feeling the twin bones of his forearm acutely, and forced his hand to knock one more time. Then I let go as quickly as I could, because touching Ted felt like playing chicken with a semi-truck.

"You okay?" he asked.

"Huh? Yeah. Of course. Just, you know, it's a witch thing."

He pretended to buy that, took his hot cup of coffee, and headed to his corner booth.

Grim plopped down at my feet with a loud exhale like a deflating air mattress. *"Do you want to talk about the fact that the walk here is lined by death and* destruction, or should we just ignore it for a while and you get me a plate of bacon?"

"You noticed?"

"Yes, I noticed. You know who else will notice before long?"

"I know, I know."

"I don't think you do. Once people realize that the path leads from the Deadwoods straight to where I live, will my life as a walking death omen become easier or harder, you think?

I rolled my eyes. "You're really making this about you?"

"Obviously. What, are you upset because you wanted to make this about you?"

"Maybe. I'm the one that's responsible for fixing it."

"You say that, but somehow I know I'm going to be dragged into it, too."

I sighed. "Okay, how many pieces for you to shut up about it until the end of my shift?"

"However much you have back there plus one."

"Fine. No bacon for—"

"Six is a good start."

I scribbled the order on my pad and dropped it off at the back for Anton. There was no way I was going to make it through this shift without being reminded again and again about the night before.

Why did I answer the door? It was such a stupid mistake. Maybe if I hadn't, whatever entity had knocked would've disappeared and no one would be the wiser.

As Tanner chatted it up with Zoe Clementine and her magic tutor, Oliver Bridgewater, I went to take Ted's order.

But once I got there, instead of asking what he wanted to eat (I already knew it would be a well-done steak and scrambled eggs, but he seemed to appreciate the option to change his order every morning, even though he never used it), I slid into the booth across from him. "Ted, I have to tell you, there's a rumor that you killed a bunch of plants last night."

His shock at me sitting down was only heightened by my statement. He stared at me silently through the black pits of his eyeholes. "Uh, no. I was building the fireproof birdhouses all night. Like I told you. Why would I want to kill a bunch of plants? I love plants. I have a garden of night veil bushes, bull nettles, wormwood, and white oleanders that I maintain on a daily basis. It's quite lovely. You're welcome to come pick from it if you ever need it for your magic."

"I didn't think you did it, either," I said, ignoring his offer. "Do you know anyone, or anything, that might've, though?"

"Might've what?"

"Wilted a bunch of plants. Like a demon or, I don't know, anything else from the Deadwoods?"

He cocked his hooded head. "I'm not an expert on it, but there are all *kinds* of things in the Deadwoods that would do that. Honestly, I don't even know where to start. And even if I did, I would probably only list one percent of the possibilities. By and large, the Deadwoods haven't been properly cataloged by Eastwind's cryptozoologists, toxicologists, or mythobiologists. The stigma around it keeps them away. I see new creatures I don't have a name for on a daily basis out there, just on my evening strolls."

The image of a grim reaper strolling solo through the Deadwoods provided a concise explanation of why Eastwind's scientific community was reluctant to venture into the Deadwoods.

"Okay. Thanks, Ted. For what it's worth, I knew it wasn't you. I just thought you should know people were talking about the event and your name came up."

"I appreciate it, but don't worry about me, Nora. I'm used to being the scapegoat for every unexplained ill in Eastwind."

"Sorry to hear it."

I stood up just as he added, "Ever had any interest in building birdhouses? I could use an extra hand, if—"

I cringed apologetically. "Super swamped in here right now. Gotta go check on some tables. Thanks for the chat."

"No, thank *you*."

"Steak and scrambled eggs, right?"

"Heh. You know me so well, Nora."

Yikes.

I scurried away.

"What was *that* about?" Tanner said, following me into the kitchen.

"Long story." I stuck Ted's order into the turnstile for Anton, who grunted. I wasn't sure what that particular grunt meant, but as long as the ogre wasn't swinging his metal burger flipper at me, I figured that was all right.

Tanner had planted himself in my way. "I got time."

"Okay, fine. But in the manager's office."

A devilish smile tweaked the corner of his mouth. "If you insist."

Once we were in the manager's office, I pushed him

NOVA NELSON

away from me as he moved closer. "No time for that. Do you want me to fill you in or not? We have a full house out there and nobody's waiting on them while we're in here."

His eyebrows shot up toward his hairline. "Oh, you *actually* have something to talk about? I thought it was just an excuse to ... No. Right. What's up?"

I caught him up to speed, and when I finished, he squinted at me like more useful information might be found in my pores. "That does seem strange. You said it was plants, right?"

"Yep."

"Sounds like you might want to talk to a West Wind witch."

"You mean like I'm doing right now?" Sometimes it seemed like Tanner completely forgot he was a witch.

"A better West Wind witch than me. I was a terrible student. I'm pretty sure they only let me graduate because they felt sorry for me and didn't want to deal with me anymore."

For some reason, it'd never occurred to me that Tanner had done the Mancer Academy thing. Obviously he had—all the witches that grew up here had to—but he never mentioned it.

"Why are you looking at me like that?" he asked. "I had a lot going on at the time. I was working two jobs, taking classes—"

"No, it's not that. I just never hear you talk about that part of your life. But, duh, of course you had your crazy teen and early twenties phrase."

He shrugged a single shoulder. "They weren't that crazy. I was too busy to do the social scene. Donovan was

54

the only close friend I made and kept from school. The rest weren't so big on how much time I spent around werewolves and shifters. Witches can be kind of snooty. And it was even worse only ten years ago."

"So who should I talk to about my problem?"

"Have you met Oliver?"

"Oliver? Zoe's tutor?"

"Yep. He graduated top in my class. Total nerd, but a good guy."

"Not one of the snooty ones?"

"Maybe a little bit. But he was mostly too buried in books to do the social scene himself. I'm sure he could help point you in the right direction."

Anton started grunting loudly from the kitchen and Tanner perked up. "Shoot. There's gotta be plates ready to go."

I hurried after him, and once the food was delivered and Anton was subdued, I took Tanner's advice and approached Zoe and Oliver.

If I'd passed Oliver on the street, the first thing I shouted at him would not be "nerd." And not just because I'm not a bully and shouting things at people you pass on the streets is lunatic behavior. More likely, and assuming I'd had a few drinks so that I forgot all my manners, I'd probably shout something more along the lines of, "Where are you headed, and can I come?"

I wasn't sure if it was something in the water supply, but the men of Eastwind were, by and large, abnormally smoking hot. Even the nerds, apparently.

Don't get me wrong, I was fully invested in seeing this Tanner thing through and, in my humble opinion, Tanner was the most jaw-droppingly gorgeous of them all, but being surrounded by so many beautiful men on a daily basis could really put a smile on a girl's face. Or a guy's face, depending.

Bottom line, if Zoe wasn't actively pursuing this tutor of hers, she and I needed to have a long talk.

Tanner was just a few steps behind me after he'd dropped off two pieces of pie for the Flannerys.

"Hey, Nora!" Zoe said. "I wanted to say hi earlier, but you're so busy. I'm glad you came by, though. Have you met Oli?"

"Not yet, though I've heard all about him." I offered my hand. "Nora Ashcroft."

"Oliver Bridgewater. Nice to meet you."

"He's helping me study for my witch's certification. I had it in Avalon, of course, but the laws here are so different, I have to pass a new exam," Zoe said cheerfully.

Tanner jumped in. "Nora has a question I thought you might be able to help with, Oliver."

"What's that?"

"It's just hypothetical," I said quickly. "I've just been hearing gossip, and you know how unreliable that is, but then it got me thinking, and I talked with Ted and he didn't know, so I asked Tanner and he said you would be the one to speak with. You know, just so I can settle this hypothetical question in my mind."

Oliver cocked his head to the side expectantly. "And that question is?"

"Right. Um, say you're just sitting at home, and you hear a knock on your front door. Three knocks."

His eyes narrowed and he leaned slightly forward. "Uh-huh?"

"And then you open the door and, well, things sort of

get blown everywhere. And the hot water you were boiling for tea disappears. And then the next day some of the plants around town have randomly withered and died. Would you say those two things are probably related, or could they be totally a coincidence? And if they're related, what would you say, hypothetically, caused all of it?"

Oliver didn't reply right away. I saw his chest rise and fall as he took a few steadying breaths. "I can't say right off the top of my head, but were this ever-so-hypothetical situation to arise, I would immediately report it to the Coven."

"Report it to the Coven?" I asked. "Like how?"

"You're new in Eastwind like Zoe, right?"

"Much newer than her, but yes."

"Then you could probably just tell one of your recertification instructors and they could report it for you."

I grimaced. "So, what if I don't have any instructors? Hypothetically. Who would I report it to then?"

"Wait," he said quickly, his eyes darting from Zoe to Tanner then to me. "You don't have an instructor? Not even a Coven-approved tutor?"

"It's hypothetical," I protested. But he wasn't buying it. He hadn't bought it since the moment the word "hypothetical" popped from my mouth.

"Okay, fine. Hypothetically, you absolutely need a Coven-approved instructor to get you certified. Or at least a Coven-approved tutor."

"I have Ruby True."

He laughed dryly. "Yeah, I don't know if the Coven will count her."

"It's not that big of a deal," I said. "I'm not running around waving my wand at things."

His eyes grew large. "You have a wand?"

"No! Well, not yet. It's on order."

When he shut his eyes and pinched the bridge of his nose, none of us spoke, and then, finally, he sat up straight again. "Okay. I'll do it."

"You'll do what?" Tanner asked.

"I'll let the Coven know about this hypothetical."

"No!" Tanner and I said at the same time.

"Please don't," I added. "It's no big deal."

"True," said Oliver. "The bigger deal here is that there's an untrained Fifth Wind witch who's only a few weeks away from getting a wand. I assume the Coven has contacted you about enrolling in training, though, right?"

"Not that I know of."

That seemed to puzzle him as he jerked his head back, creating a slight double chin. "That doesn't make sense."

I shrugged. "Maybe they don't want me in the Coven. I'm just a Fifth Wind witch, after all. I can't do any useful magic. I probably won't even be able to use my wand."

He waved it off. "No, that can't be right. How about this? I'll speak with the Coven on your behalf and convince them to let me become your private tutor, like I am for Zoe."

"I don't think that's necessary," Tanner said.

"Yeah," Zoe added. "Private lessons seem a little overkill."

"I don't have time," I said. "I work here from dawn till mid-afternoon, six or seven days a week, then I have lessons with Ruby."

"We'll find time," Oliver said. "I can come to your place whenever you finish your lessons with Ruby each night."

Tanner made a strange choking sound then said, "Seems super unnecessary, Oliver."

"Exactly," said Zoe. "Plus, we start our lessons so early some mornings, you can't stay up all night giving Nora one-on-one attention."

"Zoe has a point," Tanner said. They nodded at each other firmly.

It wasn't hard to figure out why Tanner and Zoe were such opponents to the idea, but also, I agreed with them. Just not for the same reason. I didn't need one more thing on my plate, but I knew Oliver wouldn't let up until I agreed, and the last thing I wanted was for the Coven's first impression of me to have anything to do with letting in an evil entity that may or may not have something to do with ruining people's prized gardens.

"Okay, Oliver," I said. "We can plan some lessons. But it'll have to be modified because I just don't have the time."

"Absolutely," he said, relief bolstering his smooth voice. "I'll talk to the Coven and see if I can pull some strings. Maybe we can get away with just teaching you the basics and letting Ruby provide supplemental instruction based on your specialty."

"Great. Now to answer my hypothetical?"

"Right." He tapped his lips with the tip of his finger. "You should talk to Ansel. Have him take a look at the plants, see if he can't offer any more information about what happened. That might point you in the right direction."

"You've been very helpful," I said, disguising the sarcasm as best I could.

As Tanner and I walked away, I grumbled so that only he could hear. "Good call. I got a recommendation to do something I could've thought of myself and a tutor I don't want."

"You can always cancel the tutoring," he suggested. "I don't think you need it."

Of course I needed it. But I understood why Tanner didn't love the idea of Oliver and me spending alone time with each other. After all, I was only human.

Figuratively speaking.

Chapter Six

"It's not dead," Ansel said as he examined the specimen Tanner and I brought with us to the garden center. "Or rather, it *wasn't* dead, till you picked it." He glanced up at Tanner and me. "Nice job. Anyway, it just needed a lot of water and the right kind of care. With both of those, it could have pulled through."

"What caused it, you think?" I asked.

He shrugged. "Considering it's the end of June, I'd normally go with drought, but this is an *eremortis domestica*. It's bred to be drought resistant. We have a bunch of them here that are just fine with the weather. I can show you if you like. We keep them with the cacti and succulents because they plant well with those."

I'd once seen Ansel fight on the losing end of a battle with a determined and thrashing cactus, so I wasn't keen to get within fifty feet of that section if I could help it. "It's fine, I believe you. Any guesses on what happened, then, if not the weather?"

He examined the plant again, exhaling deeply. "I

can't say. It looks like drought. That's my best guess despite the reasons contrary. It really looks like someone just sucked the water right out of it. Did you try watering it before you brought it here?"

"Nope."

He narrowed his eyes at me. "You don't know much about gardening, do you?"

"Always had a black thumb." I shrugged. "Guess it comes with the death witch gig."

Ansel turned his attention to Tanner. "And you? What's your excuse for not trying to water a wilted plant before pronouncing it dead and ripping it from its roots? You're a West Wind witch, right?"

Tanner held up his hands defensively. "I just figured, under the circumstances, that it was probably a goner."

"Under the *circumstances*?" Ansel cast a suspicious eye on me. "Care to enlighten?"

"Not so much," I said.

He crossed his arms over his dark, bare chest—I had yet to see him with his shirt on at work—and waited patiently for me to explain myself.

"Fine," I said. "But you can't tell anyone."

"I'm going to tell Jane," he said flatly.

"Fine, you can tell Jane. But that's it."

He nodded once, indicating that I should get on with it already.

"Some dark entity visited me at Ruby's house last night, and then this morning there was a path of withered plants leading away from her porch and into the Deadwoods." I said it as quickly as I could so the admission was like ripping off a Band-Aid.

Ansel threw his head back and laughed, and his

bulging biceps relaxed as his arms fell to his sides. "You're trouble, you know that?" He addressed Tanner next. "I hope you know what you're getting into, dating this one."

"We're not dating," I said weakly.

He rolled his eyes at me. "Right. Anyway, if this actually has anything to do with a dark entity, I'm out. It's way beyond my pay grade. Admittedly, I don't know much about witches or care to know much about you folks, but this has 'witchcraft' written all over it. Your best bet is to find a witch who knows what she's talking about and solve this the sorcery way."

"Ansel," Tanner said, "don't you think we've already thought of that? It was Oliver Bridgewater who told us to come see you."

"Oliver?" Ansel said. "The nerdy one?"

"Yep."

"And what kind of witch is he?"

"West Wind," said Tanner. "Like me, except way smarter."

"Ah, there's your problem," Ansel said, wiping beads of sweat from the side of his neck. "This isn't a soil issue, so it's not a West Wind problem. If the rest of the affected plants are anything like this *eremortis domestica,* they're in need of water. I'd say you best find yourself a East Wind witch to help." He squinted at something over my shoulder. "Thaddeus just poked his head out of the shop. I better look busy. You two completely platonic friends have fun with your adventure. Hope I helped."

As Ansel traipsed through the thick foliage and disappeared from our sight where we stood on the walkway, I turned to Tanner. "Should we go to the

Coven with this?" I said. "I don't know any East Wind witches who could help us."

He stared at me strangely, like my sanity was up for debate. "Yes, you do."

"But who do—" Then it clicked. "Oh. Nope. Can't happen. He hates me. I could beg him to help and he'd refuse."

Tanner nodded along. "Probably true. But if I asked, I know he would say yes."

I groaned. "Please don't make me work with him on this."

"I'll be there to keep the peace, don't worry."

I wanted to say, *Like you kept the peace at Sheehan's?* But it was physically impossible for me to be mean to Tanner. Sometimes I wondered if there was something magical protecting him from meanness—no joke. No one was ever rude to him. It was unsettling, truth be told. Even when Donovan had caught Tanner and me kissing by the bathrooms, while his response dripped with disdain, his words themselves were actually a compliment: *I just think you can do a lot better.*

"Fine, but do me a favor and make it clear to Donovan that I am against this plan from the start."

"Fine, fine." Tanner put his arm around my shoulder and we started down the path, heading out of the garden center and toward Ruby's house.

Maybe it could work out okay as long as Tanner was there actively mediating. Maybe sharing a common goal with Donovan would divert his focus away from his inexplicable hatred of me and toward something more productive. Then, who knew, maybe I could show him that I'm not whatever awful thing he imagined me to be.

First, of course, I would have to figure out what that thing was. Then I would have to make sure I wasn't it.

Ugh. I was such an idiot. Why did I care about whether or not Donovan Stringfellow liked me? With few exceptions, I never cared about that kind of thing. I was Nora Freaking Ashcroft, self-made woman and restaurateur! Not only that, I was Nora Freaking Ashcroft, self-made witch, survivor of death, and co-owner of the most successful all-night diner in town! I'd done the whole self-made thing twice. *Twice!* And I was the first to admit that working hard and building something for yourself meant leaving a lot of bitter people in your wake. It hadn't bothered me before, so why did it bother me now?

Was it because Donovan was Tanner's best friend, and having the best friend dislike me put my relationship with Tanner in jeopardy over the long term?

Sure. I'd go with that. It was respectable enough.

Plus, I was afraid that if I dug deeper, I'd unearth something I wasn't as comfortable believing.

Grim was easy to spot as we passed the long row of attached homes leading up to Ruby's porch. Normally, the overgrown rosemary bushes in Ruby's garden would have obscured him from view in his favorite spot.

But.

Yeah, not currently a problem, and his bulky black form stood out against the painted blue wood of the porch.

His hulking presence *almost* distracted from the old necromancer on the porch swing wearing a stern frown as she rocked back and forth with a dead wormwood plant spread across her lap.

"Hi, Ms. True," Tanner said cheerily, but his voice wavered slightly. Also, he never called her Ms. True. They were on a first-name basis by now.

Tanner was nervous.

And why wouldn't he be with the way she glared at us? Well, at *me*.

"Well, look who it is," Ruby said as I paused at the bottom of the stairs. She rocked in the swing in a precise rhythm as she spoke.

"I've been working on it," I said, trying to cut her off at the pass.

"And yet"—she grabbed the tea kettle from beside her, which I hadn't noticed, my full attention having been on her angry expression—"still no tea." She removed the lid and tilted the kettle so I could see the empty insides. "Every time I fill it up, it goes right back down."

Holy shifter, this was not good. Ruby's tea was like a sacrament for her. And the fact that my dumb actions had deprived her of it for an entire day did *not* bode well for my living situation. "I'm sorry," I said.

Her voice became sweet like antifreeze. "Don't be sorry, dear." Then her soft expression faded. "Just fix it, for fang's sake, before I *do* decide to raise an army of the dead and take out this boring and gossipy town once and for all!"

I glanced cautiously at Tanner, whose wide eyes were glued to Ruby. What was the beverage equivalent of hangry? Whatever it was, Ruby was rocking it right now, so much so that she didn't care if the neighbors heard her talking about raising an army of the dead.

"I promise I'm working on it, Ruby. And I'm going to keep working on it as soon as I get off my shift tomorrow."

Tanner hurriedly stepped up onto the first stair. "I'll give her the morning off," he blurted.

"What?" I said, whipping my head toward him. "I don't need—"

"That's a start," Ruby replied, but she did sound mildly subdued.

"That way Nora can get to work on it as soon as she wakes up. We've already decided which East Wind witch she should talk to, so it'll be fixed right away."

"Not soon enough," Ruby said, shaking her empty kettle.

"Bring your favorite tea to Medium Rare tomorrow and I'll brew you a cup. And throw in some bacon, no charge. How about that?"

Oh, he was *good*. More than that. Tanner was a miracle maker.

The corners of Ruby's mouth twitched, and I was sure she was about to crack a smile. "Yes, that will suffice for now." Then she stood and marched inside.

I rounded on Tanner. "How are you going to find someone to cover for my shift this late?"

"Details," he said, running his hands down my arms. "And the prospect of running the entire diner on my own tomorrow morning is much less frightening than letting you sleep in a house with Ruby when she's that upset. She's been known to lash out when her routine is disrupted."

"Really?" With the exception of what I just saw, Ruby had always seemed to run on an even keel. Then again, I'd never seen her tea rituals disrupted before. So maybe Tanner had a point.

"Yeah. This could be just another rumor, but I heard

that one of the reasons she never officially joined the Coven was because they scheduled morning lessons when she usually ate breakfast. They tried to make her go anyway, and she cursed all of them with sleep paralysis for a week until they gave in."

"Mm-hm. Yeah, I'll take tomorrow off."

"Great. I'll send an owl to Donovan. He usually works evenings, so he should be available tomorrow morning. I'll catch him up to speed and tell him to be nice to you."

Like that would work.

I groaned. "Do I have to?"

"Yes."

"Don't you know another East Wind witch we can ask?"

Tanner shrugged. "Sure. I know plenty of East Wind witches. But Donovan's the only one I trust to not only keep this low-key, but also keep you safe."

I doubted that last bit but decided not to rain on Tanner's parade. Maybe Donovan's loyalty to his best friend would outweigh his distaste for me. After all, he'd kept it quiet about what he saw at Sheehan's when that could have just as easily been the talk of the town for at least a day and a half until some new minor scandal cropped up.

"Fine."

"He's a good guy," Tanner said. "You two just got off on the wrong foot when he thought you were framing me for Bruce's murder."

"That'll do it," I said. "Is holding grudges a East Wind witch thing?"

Tanner laughed. "No, but admittedly, it *is* a Donovan

thing. The flip side of it is that when he's loyal, he's really freaking loyal."

"Fine, fine. I'll go see him tomorrow morning." I hollered up to the patio. "You hear that, Grim? You're coming with me bright and early. No excuses."

"Over my dead body."

I grinned at Tanner. "Perfect. Grim is one hundred percent in."

"Let me know how it goes afterward, okay?"

"Of course."

"Lunch on me. You can bring Donovan with you, if you want."

"Oh great! A lunch date with my favorite witch," I said sarcastically.

Tanner flashed me his confident half-grin. "You better watch out, Nora Ashcroft. Donovan Stringfellow is Eastwind's most eligible heartbreaker. I would hate to see you fall victim."

"There's only one person I'm likely to fall victim to." And then, much to Grim's vocal disapproval from his spot on the patio, I leaned forward and snuck a quick kiss from Tanner before heading inside.

* * *

"This has necromancy written all over it," Ruby said from her overstuffed chair in the corner of the parlor. She closed a book called *Shift Work* and set it aside as I entered, took my place at the parlor table (I really needed to invest in a comfy chair for myself), and waited for the lecture to commence.

Ruby didn't disappoint. "My best guess is that it's

shoddy necromancy of something powerful. The attack was targeted, but the entity's heart wasn't into it. I was able to banish it without much effort, but its powerful signature still lingers."

"So what does that mean for us?"

She wagged a finger at me. "Oh, no, you don't. There's no us in this. Only you."

"*Samesies,*" said Grim from the hearth.

"*Nice try. As my familiar, my problems are also your problems.*"

"*Does it work both ways? Because I've had this dryness right below my tail that—*"

"*Definitely doesn't work both ways.*"

I returned my attention to Ruby. "Fine. What's this mean for me?"

"A powerful entity controlled by weak necromancy? I'd say that it spells trouble. Big trouble. And I'd be surprised if you were the only one it affected. No, whatever this is could shake loose from its summoner without much effort, if it hasn't already."

"Yet again, I'm in awe of your ability to instill confidence in your pupil," I said. "So what do you recommend I do?"

"Speaking with the East Wind witch would be my recommendation, too. I assume someone else came up with that idea for you."

I resented her assumption that I couldn't come up with good ideas myself, but also, she was right.

"Ansel suggested it."

She perked up, surprised. "Oh yeah? And how many Coven-trained witches did you ask before a werebear had to be the one to talk sense?" She sighed exasperatedly. "Don't answer that. It'll only depress me."

I wasn't in love with the tea-deprived version of Ruby.

Grim, on the other hand, wagged his tail lethargically with each of her pointed jabs, slapping the creaky floorboards.

"Anywho, Ansel's right. You'll need to combine elemental forces with the hydromancer. There's a connection ritual you can do that will combine both your magics."

"A connection ritual?" With Donovan?

Maybe, with time, I could learn to love this new cranky version of Ruby. It would be easier than whatever she was suggesting, I was certain.

"That sounds like more intimacy than I care to have with Donovan Stringfellow."

"*Donovan Stringfellow?*" Ruby said, blinking rapidly. "*That's* the hydromancer you're going to see?" She whistled low. "If I were thirty years younger—heck, maybe just five years younger—I would conjure an evil entity solely to have an excuse to combine magic with that young man."

"Ew. Too far. Also, he hates me, so I can't imagine him agreeing to something that sounds almost as intimate as sex."

"Nora, dear, combining magic is vastly more intimate than sex. You'll know when you try it."

I served her up a heaping plate of side eye. "You're really not selling this for me."

"The Stringfellows are powerful witches, Nora. If you want to contain this dark force, Donovan's a good bet.

I once combined powers with his grandfather, Haverford Stringfellow. An aeromancer, that one. We managed to stop a siege of undead pixies, if I do recall."

"Noted. And I'm gonna need to hear that full story later, but for now, I feel like we should have the equivalent of a birds-and-bees talk for combining magic."

"It's not that hard. It comes naturally to you. When two witches want to control a powerful force, they simply join hands recite a few incantations around a cauldron, and the magics blend. It's a mini version of being part of a circle."

"What's a circle? Is that like, um"—I hesitated but couldn't think of a better comparison—"group sex?"

"Usually less satisfying. But sure, the simile holds well enough."

"Are you part of a circle?" I tried not to think about it.

She waved that away. "Hellhound, no. The Coven practically begged me to join so that they could have their first complete circle in over a century, but I wouldn't give them the pleasure."

"What do you mean, first complete circle?"

"The term 'circle' is used loosely. It's actually a pentagram. Each point of the star represents one of the core elements—earth, air, water, fire—plus the one that runs through them all, the spirit. A complete circle contains one of each type of wind—the aeromancers of the North Wind, whose powers are strongest in the winter; the pyromancers of the South Wind, whose powers are strongest in the summer; the terramancers of the West Wind, strongest in the autumn; the hydromancers of the East Wind, who named this town and are at their magical peak in the spring. And, of course, the necromancers of the Fifth Wind who are miserable year round.

"Since you and I are the only Fifth Wind witches in recent memory, the Coven has been forced to form incomplete circles. They still work for most things, but a circle that harnesses all the winds could easily rule the Coven and, by extension, Eastwind. That was a power I had no desire to impart upon any of the circles currently in play back when the Coven was courting me so relentlessly."

"Now I feel kind of lousy that the Coven hasn't approached me to join."

Ruby chuckled dryly. "Don't take it too hard. I'm sure they're aware of your presence in town, and the fact that they haven't started knocking on our door every day likely means they want you so badly, they're afraid to scare you off. And it makes sense."

"What makes sense?"

She paused, and her hesitation weighed heavy in the air. "You're more powerful than you know, Nora. You've only just begun to discover it, but if your accidental channeling was any indication, you have many more surprises on the way. Speaking of which, are you still wearing that amulet?"

I pulled it by the chain out from underneath my boat-neck tee, revealing the staurolite cross.

"And you're recharging it daily?"

"Just like you showed me."

"Good. You'll want to make sure you stay on that until you're sure this dark entity is gone."

I tucked it away again. "Oliver insists I register with the Coven. What do you think?"

"Oh sure, why not?"

I paused. "Um, that's what I'm asking you. You don't have the highest opinion of them."

"Be that as it may, I don't think they can, or would, do anything to you. You're valuable to them, even if they haven't started badgering you yet. Register or don't. It doesn't matter."

"Will they ask me to join a circle?"

"I assume so."

"And then what do I say?"

"Whatever the fang you want!" Ruby groaned. "It's like you're backsliding in our training. Listen to your Insight and do what it tells you."

"Right, right. Geez. Cranky. Oliver also says I need to take lessons from the Coven."

"Oh, well *that's* a load of unicorn swirls. You don't need your Insight to tell you that."

"He was adamant that he tutor me."

Ruby thought about it, her gaze drifting up to the baubles hanging from the ceiling. Every so often one would start moving out of nowhere, and I wasn't sure I'd ever get used to that. I supposed it meant they were working, guarding us from whatever strange entities were causing them to sway.

Or that's what I told myself to be able to sleep at night. As far as white lies went, it seemed like a keeper.

"Oliver Bridgewater, right?" she said, finally.

"Yes. He's currently Zoe Clementine's tutor."

She tapped a wrinkled finger to her lips. "It might not hurt for you to have a few lessons from him. If it keeps the Coven out of our hair, we can work our schedule around it. I hate teaching the basic lessons anyway—protection spells, levitation, healing potions. All a bore. He could take over those, and I can stick with the good stuff. Then I have more time for my reading. After all, I'm retired."

She grabbed her book again and flipped it open.

In her mind at least, the matter was clearly settled, a plan in place. Nothing more to consider.

Easy for her to believe. She wasn't the one that would have to swap magic with Donovan the next day.

Chapter Seven

I knocked on the bright blue front door and waited, heart pounding in my chest. The house was two blocks outside the cluster of buildings surrounding Fulcrum Park, but because it was only six thirty in the morning, the street was silent except for the trickle of the water garden in the front yard. I would have preferred to sleep in on my day off work, but I knew it was best for everyone if Grim and I made it out the door before Ruby awoke and remembered that she was unable to brew her own tea.

I thought about knocking again. What if he didn't answer? That would be just like Donovan to leave me waiting on his doorstep, to agree to meet with me and then be nowhere around when the time came.

"Maybe he's dead," Grim suggested from beside me.

"Don't get my hopes up."

"I don't know why that would. You know as well as I do that death isn't always the end of the story. Some of us can't catch a break."

The door swung open, and Donovan stared

impassively at me before his eyes traveled down to my feet and back up to my head like he was scanning for all the bits about me he could detest.

Appearance-wise, he was not at his peak. His dark hair, which was usually well-styled, short but swept back and to the side hadn't gotten any attention. His white T-shirt was wrinkled and twisted, suggesting he'd slept in it. His jeans lacked a belt and sagged, showing the top elastic of his briefs and a sliver of his olive skin just above that.

"You're a morning person, aren't you?" he said distastefully.

"Not by choice. But I *am* an adult, so I learned how to pull it together before noon."

He rolled his eyes. "I work late. Not everyone has the luxury of getting off work at three p.m. to run around town, solving everyone's problems and becoming Eastwind's favorite death witch."

"Aww," I said. "Thanks. It's good to be loved." I pushed past him and into his dark house, and Grim followed a step behind me.

"Not sure Gustav's going to like having a dog inside."

"Gustav? Is that your familiar?"

"Obviously."

"Well, Gustav doesn't have to worry, because Grim isn't a dog. He's a grim."

Donovan shut the door behind me. "You really went all out with the creative naming."

"It's a gift," I said, looking around. Donovan's home spoke of a deep passion for interior decorating. The fact that he was particular about his environment didn't surprise me. His talent did, though.

The vibe wasn't unlike that of Atlantis Day Spa, with candles floating in midair, and the peaceful trickle of flowing water echoing somewhere in the background. An aquarium served as one of the walls in the living room, and a candelabra behind it cast watery reflections throughout the space.

"There's no way this guy is straight," said Grim.

"Easy on the stereotypes."

"You saying I'm wrong?"

"I'm just reserving judgment."

To be fair, Grim raised an interesting point, and my mind jumped back to Donovan's comment when he caught Tanner and I kissing, the one about how Tanner could do so much better. Was he referring to himself as the better option?

Wow. That actually made a lot of sense. Not that it mattered one way or another, but maybe Donovan was gay. Huh.

"Tea?" he asked. "Or are you the kind to want a stiff drink first thing in the morning?"

"Do I seem like that type to you?"

He pooched out his lips, thinking way too hard about it, in my opinion. "Nah. You're too tightly wound to be someone who starts her day with a shot. I'll brew some tea."

As he shuffled into the other room, I tried not to fixate on his comment about me being tightly wound.

After all, I wasn't. Not even a little bit. Was I? No. I was totally relaxed. If anyone was tightly wound, it was him.

His living room lacked traditional furniture. Instead, he'd placed cushions on the ground around a low stone table, at the center of which water bubbled from a small crater. Grim flopped down in the darkest corner he could find.

Dang. Donovan didn't take this East Wind witch thing lightly. Maybe I *had* come to the right place for help, despite my personal issues with him.

I ran my finger through the mini fountain in the table, just to make sure it was real. Every so often things I took for granted in Eastwind would turn out to be magical illusions, and I'd developed a habit of checking whenever possible. Not only was the water real, but it was warm and soothing, sending relaxation through my arm and into my shoulder.

I'd experienced that only once before. Again, at Atlantis Day Spa. Right before Frankie the Nix tried to drown me.

I shouldn't have been surprised that Donovan's entire house was a trigger for me to relive some of my worst moments. Maybe next he would turn on some Xana choral music and ask me to go for a drive at night through Nowhere, Texas.

Emerging from the kitchen, he carried a bamboo tray with a teapot and two tiny cups covered in ornate hand-painted cherry blossoms that added a tally mark in the "probably gay" column of the mental score card I was now keeping. A charcoal gray cat with raised and pointed ears followed at his heels and arched its back when Grim lifted his head in the corner to get a sniff. "Easy, Gustav," Donovan said, setting the tray on the low table before easing down onto a cushion opposite mine.

He poured two cups but made me reach rather than handing it to me. I stared down at it. This was definitely not the same type of tea Ruby brewed on a daily basis. I couldn't tell the color in the dim lighting and with the black ceramic cup, but judging by the smell, I guessed it was a green tea.

"It's not poison," he said, sipping his. "Tanner would kill me if I poisoned you."

"I'm going to pretend that's not the only reason you wouldn't poison me." I sipped the tea, and it was actually delightful. Lighter than I would've preferred this early in the day, but the taste was much less bitter than what Ruby brewed ... back when she could keep water in the kettle.

"Tanner filled me in a little bit," he said, "but he left out some key details. Most importantly, how did the entity get into your house?"

His intense stare penetrated me, and I knew that he probably had a pretty good idea of how the entity made it in. So I decided to come clean. He already thought I was a tightly wound idiot. Might as well speed up the process here so I could move on with my day. "I let it in. It knocked three times, and I was preoccupied with something else, and opened the door."

"Scratch multitasking off your list of possible skills."

"I get it. You think I'm worthless. Can we move on?"

He blinked, his head jerking minutely to the side. "I don't think that."

"You just imply it. All the time. Moving on."

He sighed and set down his cup. "I think the best bet is to perform a clarity ritual. If it works."

"Why wouldn't it work?"

"Have you ever done a clarity ritual?"

"No."

"Do you even know what a clarity ritual is?"

"Not exactly, but I—"

"That's why it might not work."

I threw back the rest of my tea and set the empty cup on the table a little harder than necessary. "Okay, you win."

"I'm just saying, you might have magic in you, but using magic is a skill to be learned. And since you haven't bothered to get any proper training—"

"Ruby's been tutoring me."

"Yeah, I said *proper* training. I just don't have high expectations for this."

"Then let's hope confidence isn't essential for this to work."

He scooted over to the cushion next to mine. "I'm the leader, here, okay?"

I opened my eyes wide and nodded emphatically. "Yes, sir." I could tell it got under his skin by the minute flair of his nostrils.

"A clarity ritual, if not totally botched by an unskilled and obstinate witch, will open up a window to the timeless, meaning we can see things in any time and any space."

"That seems intense."

"It is. I absolutely should not be doing it with you, and if you tell anyone I did, I'll deny it to the grave. That being said, it's the most direct path to learning what we need to get this entity out of Eastwind and back to wherever it came from, and therefore it's the quickest way to get you out of my house so I can go back to bed. And again, this is assuming it works at all."

"Okay, great. What's the worst that can happen?"

"Never ask that." He shut his eyes and ran his hands through the water at the center of the table, rubbing it around until his skin glistened. "Soak your hands," he said, and I did without any further questions.

Did I trust Donovan?

Duh, no.

But we had a shared goal of figuring out what I'd let into Ruby True's apartment, and sometimes a shared goal was the best one could hope for in an ally.

"Don't you need your wand or something?" I asked.

He glared at me. "No. Not for this. Stop asking questions. Now hold my hands." He held his out to me.

"Wait, is this ... a connection ritual?" I remembered what Ruby had said about it being more intimate than sex.

"I said no more questions, but yes."

My heart jumped into my throat.

He exhaled, dropped his hands before I could grab them, and said, "For fang's sake, Nora. I can feel the tension coming off you from here. It won't work unless you relax."

"Yeah, sorry."

He cocked his head to the side, examining me. "Hold on. You've heard about the connection ritual?"

I nodded.

"Ah. So you know it's a little ... intense."

"Intimate was the word Ruby used."

A sly grin bloomed on his face before he tucked it away again. "That's a good word for it."

"Is this going to be ... weird?"

"*Oh* yeah. Tanner wasn't happy about it."

"Then once it's done, can we never speak of it again?" I asked.

"That's the plan." He wet his hands again and I did the same. And this time, when he held out his hands, I grabbed them, feeling the relaxing warmth of the water between our skin, and shut my eyes.

Donovan began murmuring in a deep drone. I didn't know this language, but it felt familiar. It also sounded not unlike the one Ruby had used to send the dark entity from her home.

So, yeah, I could benefit from a little formal schooling in the witchcraft department.

I let my mind settle into the present, calling upon the meditation techniques I'd learned in my past life.

And ... nothing.

"It feels like there's something blocking your energy," he said.

I opened my eyes. "You mean besides my lack of training?"

He kept his eyes shut and nodded. "Yeah, it's like a wall. I can't even find your energy. I could find the energy on a simple post owl if I needed to." He let go of my hands and opened his eyes. "Do you have some sort of protection on you?"

"Oh." I reached down my shirt and pulled out the staurolite amulet. "You mean something like this?"

He groaned. "Is that staurolite? Are you kidding me?"

I pulled the chain over my head and set the amulet down next to me. "My bad."

He sighed, summoning patience, and said, "Okay, let's try this again."

We went through the hand-washing thing again,

and when we joined up and he began his chant, I immediately noticed a difference. There was a flow coming from his right hand into my left, and one coming out of my right hand into his left. A cyclone of energy flowed through me, sluggish at first until he broke down any resistance in its path and became a tornado.

Then the images hit me like a tidal wave ...

The sun beating down on cracked dirt as far as the eye could see.

A black form sweeping through a lush garden, leaving nothing but wilt and death behind it.

Blinding sunlight as wooden horse-drawn carts cut twin fissures in the sand.

A natural tunnel of dark trees leading to the unknown, mist hovering around the soil.

A dark human figure appearing in the road in a small Texas town.

When I opened my eyes, I was on my back, staring at the ceiling of Donovan's living room.

Donovan's heavy breathing a few feet away filled my ears, as I raised myself carefully onto my elbows to peer down my body at him. He was on his back as well, but didn't seem in a hurry to sit up. I had the urge to climb on top, but smacked myself in the cheek a few times until that idea went away. It had to be residue from the ritual.

"I don't think it worked," I said, breaking the silence.

He sat up and stared at me with an expression I'd never seen on him before. Maybe he was suffering similar side effects as I had for the briefest moment. It certainly looked that way.

"Are you kidding? I've never had one work that well."

He narrowed his eyes at me. "I've also never done it with a Fifth Wind witch before."

"First time for everything." I forced a smile, feeling heat rise in my neck. I wished he would stop looking at me like that.

"Does Tanner know you're this powerful?" But before I could respond, he laughed dryly. "Of course he doesn't. It wouldn't matter to him anyway."

"We didn't get anything useful from it, though."

"Are you kidding? We got way more than we needed. We just don't know what it means yet. That last bit, though ..."

I froze. Had he seen the glimpse of the figure in the road? The one that had caused me to crash, die, and end up in Eastwind? That had been my little secret. I'd taken it to the grave once, and my plan was to do it again. There was something more to it, some relevance I didn't yet understand, and the last person I wanted to know about it was him. "Which part?"

"The tunnel of trees."

I let go of the breath I was holding. "Right. What about it?"

"I feel like we need to go there, like we were moving toward it. Couldn't you feel that?"

I considered it. "Yeah, you're right. It was like it was calling to us. It didn't feel like the others, either."

"Exactly. Those felt like they were in the past or the future."

"Yes!" I said excitedly. "But the tunnel felt like it was right now. Like it was calling to us from the present, through space."

He bobbed his head gently as I spoke, and I could

already see the storm clouds rolling over his mind as he gazed at the bubbling water on the table. "We only brushed the surface. There's so much more we could mine."

"Round two?" I asked, my stomach clenching at the prospect.

He nodded. "Definitely. Try to focus on the tunnel this time."

We washed our hands again and our eyes met a moment before we grabbed hold of each other.

This time, the appearance of the images was immediate. He didn't even need to chant before they blazed before my eyes. Only, they weren't so much avant-garde flashes as a continuous shot, like in a movie fast forwarded at sixteen times the speed. Even though I remained still, the vision gave me whiplash as the perspective shot forward, through familiar streets of Eastwind, past Medium Rare, and into the Deadwoods. I had a creeping suspicion that I was seeing through the eyes of the entity.

The images didn't stop once we entered the Deadwoods. We zoomed through thick oaks and firs, over slowly trickling streams, past a rickety wooden shack with birdhouses hanging from the trees, and on and on, deeper and deeper. How far did the Deadwoods stretch? What was beyond them?

It felt like my spirit was jolted from my body when the vision came to a sudden halt. And maybe it was, because I looked around, and next to me stood Donovan. Neither of us said a word, though.

We stood at the edge of the tunnel of trees, fog swirling low over the ground. On instinct, I approached the threshold, but the moment my foot crossed below the arched boughs—

I was on my back again, staring up at Donovan's ceiling while everything in my peripheral vision spun in rapid and uneven circles.

"That's not supposed to happen," groaned Donovan from the ground.

When I propped myself up on my elbows this time, my head spinning and my stomach churning, I found him flat on his back, his legs spread eagle on either side of my knees, his arms out at ninety-degree angles from his torso. He didn't bother trying to get up.

"Sheesh. Which part?" I asked, squeezing my eyes shut and using the table to pull myself up to sitting again.

"Um, most of it, actually. The continuous vision, being able to see each other. And I got the strangest feeling that I was looking through—"

"The eyes of whatever it was," I finished for him. "Yeah, I had that, too."

He groaned again then also used the table to pull himself onto his knees. "I've never heard about that happening." He massaged his temples. "Maybe it's a Fifth Wind witch thing."

"Maybe," I said. "What I do know is that I need to pay a visit to the Deadwoods."

Grim perked up in the corners, his ears pushing forward on high alert. *"Yes! 'Bout time! I can show you all the best places. The Glen of Loss, Scavenger Hill, Sorrow Creek—all the best places. You'll absolutely hate them."*

Donovan shot me near lethal side eye. "You need to go into the Deadwoods? Did you hear what you just said?"

"Yep."

"Alone?"

"No. Grim will be with me. He'll give me the tour."

"Nuh-uh. I can't let you do that."

I laughed. "It's not up to you."

"Maybe not, but I'm going to do everything in my power to stop you. I promised Tanner I wouldn't let you dive headfirst into a suicide mission. He said you have a thing for that."

"I do not!" Was Tanner really saying things like that behind my back, or was Donovan being dramatic?

"You absolutely do. But here, how about this. In all likelihood, whatever visited you was a one-time thing. That happens occasionally. Some lonely loser summons something from beyond, it does its job, then it disappears. Before we go stomping into the Deadwoods, let's wait and see if it was a one-off visit."

Yeah, I caught that. "Before *we* go stomping into the Deadwoods?"

He rolled his eyes. "Yes. We. You and me."

"And me! No way you're leaving me behind the one time you go anywhere good."

"The way I see it," Donovan continued, "if you go into the Deadwoods alone, you're as good as, well, dead. And then *I'm* as good as dead if Tanner finds out I let you go by yourself. So, if you're set on exploring the single most dangerous territory in the entire realm—"

"I am."

"And there's nothing I can do to stop you—"

"There's not."

"Then our best bet is to go in there together."

"Sounds like a plan. When do we go?"

He stood up and grabbed the tray. "Nuh-uh. You have to promise me you will not go running into the Deadwoods until we know for sure that the entity is still prowling around. Until we hear anything else, we're not going anywhere. Considering you're now dragging my life into jeopardy, I think you owe me that."

I wasn't big on him towering over me, so I stood as well. I was a few inches shorter than him, but it was better than before. "Okay, deal. But as soon as I hear about another attack—"

"*If* you hear about another attack. Which you probably won't. And please, for the love of Gaia, don't go thinking every plant that dies during the middle of the summer is a sign that it's time to storm the castle, okay?"

"Ye of little faith." He glared at me. "Yeah, okay, fine. I won't do that."

He left the room with the tea tray and when he returned a moment later, he paused in the doorway. "You're still here."

"You have to promise me one thing, too," I said.

"Nope. We're already even. I promised to go into the Deadwoods with you if you promised to wait and see if there was a second attack. Promise session over. Next item on the agenda."

"Oh, for fang's sake. Just hear me out. I need you to promise you won't tell Tanner about our plans. Or, um, about the visions."

He chuckled dryly. "You think I'd run and tell my best friend that I conducted a connection ritual not once, but twice with his girlfriend? And, oh yeah, we're planning a date to the Deadwoods to most likely get ourselves killed."

"Fair point. But I'm not his girlfriend."

Donovan arched an eyebrow at me. "Does *he* know that?"

"Yes. I mean, he should. We've never talked about it, so I just assumed—"

He held up a hand to stop me. "Please. I'm not Jane. I don't want to know all about your love life. In fact, I don't want to know anything about your love life. Now, if you don't mind, I'm going to see if I can't sleep off some of the impending headache from that brain scramble we just went through. You know where the door is, right?"

Wow. Okay. For a moment, I'd thought we were in this together. Not that we were suddenly friends, but that there was some mutual civility. But apparently not. Donovan was still a jerk who could only tolerate the sight of me for so long.

He disappeared the way he'd come, and I grabbed the amulet and led Grim toward the front door.

But not before sneaking a peek at the kitchen. It was immaculate, with copper pots and pans hung along the wall over deep blue marble countertops.

"*Still unsure?*" Grim asked as we emerged into the bright morning light.

"*Yeah, I've never seen a single straight man with a kitchen like that.*"

"*Probably because he's not a single straight man. Or at least not if Gustav is any indication.*"

"*Gustav? You mean his familiar?*"

"*Yep. Never met a gayer cat,*" said Grim.

"*I didn't know cats could be gay.*"

"*Anything can be gay, Nora. Even stuff that's not gay has the potential to be a little gay.*"

THIRD KNOCK THE CHARM

"Thanks for the wisdom. I owe you one."

"One ... steak?"

I sighed. I had the day off work and didn't particularly want to spend it *at* work. Plus, now that I had a secret to keep from Tanner, I didn't trust myself to be around him right away when the vision was still so fresh in my mind.

I couldn't go back to Ruby's house, though. Not while the mystery was unsolved and she still couldn't brew her own tea. Maybe in a few hours, once she'd had time to take Tanner up on his offer of free tea and bacon at Medium Rare, she'd be in a better mood and I could fill her in then.

What I needed was somewhere to sit and think. There were two separate questions to answer here. First, what was the thing that had entered Ruby's home, the one from our vision. But also, who had set it after me? It seemed like it would take quite a bit of power to send something like that after a person, and until I figured out who it was, I might still be at risk. It hadn't injured me in my encounter, but I'd also had Ruby there to cast it out before it had much of a chance.

Unfortunately, it looked like I would need to come up with a list of possible suspects, all of whom would share the motivation of hating me. Great. What a fun way to spend the morning off of work.

But if the person responsible was to be dealt with, my options were either catch them myself or tell Deputy Stu Manchester what had happened, thereby admitting my stupidity to him (not ideal) and being tasked with convincing him it was something criminal and, therefore, his job to solve (not likely). Deputy Manchester was a good guy at heart, but sometimes bringing him into the picture was more trouble than it was worth. This felt like one of those times. Being a witch, I was probably better equipped for this sort of situation anyway. Manchester was just a were-elk, after all. I doubt he had any proclivity for catching evil entities, and if he did, what would he even do, lock it away in Ironhelm Penitentiary? Not sure how that would work.

"How about meatballs instead?" I said.

"Only if we're talking Franco's Pizza meatballs. You can't cook worth a rat-shifter's rump."

"And yet, you still beg for scraps when I do. What does that say about your standards, Grim?"

"Nothing about my standards, everything about my desperation to get my daily nutrients."

"Grease isn't a required nutrient."

"Maybe not for you."

The idea of spending the morning at Franco's Pizza, eating Italian food and sipping a spritzer, sounded divine. As soon as I imagined it, I knew it was the right fit for the day. If I had to spend my free time thinking about who would want to send a possibly demonic entity after me, that was where I wanted to be.

Chapter Eight

My wand couldn't come soon enough.

I didn't often wish I had one—after all, I'd lived my whole life without—but while I was wiping down the empty tables and booths at Medium Rare at six fifteen in the morning, I couldn't help but think of the ease with which Donovan did his job at Franco's Pizza, thanks to his little tool.

His wand, I mean.

Like, his actual wand. Not ...

Anyway.

It would have been nice to complete it all with a flick of the wrist rather than hunching over to reach the far side of the table by the window and digging in the creases of the booth to get out all the crumbs. I had to remind myself that even once Ezra had finished my wand, I had years of training with it before I was as skilled as Donovan. And, considering I was the oh-so-special black sheep of the witch family, I might never get to that point. Who knew if I could wield a wand with any sort of power or precision. Channeling ghosts? Check. Going on vision journeys that my flunky friends from high school would pay their life savings to experience? Check. Everything else witchy? Not so much.

"How'd it go?" Tanner said, drying off his hands on his apron as he popped out of the kitchen.

"Fine. I found three spoons and a copper in the crease of the second booth from the corner. Not sure what the story is there ..."

"No," he said. "I mean, how did your meeting with Donovan go? You didn't come by for lunch, so I've been dying to hear all about it."

"Oh, right. Sorry, still a little groggy this morning." I looked around. Hendrix Hardy, the insomniac werewolf who spends more late nights and early mornings in Medium Rare than in his own home, was currently the only guest. He sipped his coffee and stared out the window toward the Deadwoods like a complete zombie. The odds of him listening to us were slim, the odds of his deprived brain retaining any of the information slimmer, but still, I didn't want to go into too much detail with Tanner, so Hendrix was the perfect excuse to keep it basic. "Yeah, it was fine."

"You find out anything useful?"

I grimaced. "Eh, not really." I nodded toward Hendrix. "We can talk later. But seriously, nothing especially interesting."

He leaned forward, speaking softly. "The, um, ritual, or whatever you did. Did that work?" He leaned back, feigning mild disinterest once the words were out. But I knew what he was getting at. Did I tell him the truth? That, yes, we did a connection ritual and it was so amazing we did it twice, and in between I was overcome with a split-second attraction for his best friend that I only just managed to reel in?

Telling him that seemed mean. You try being mean to Tanner. It's impossible. Even if what you're saying is the truth.

So, yes, I lied. I didn't think there was any practical harm in it. "Not really. And I wasn't big on trying it again with Donovan, and he wasn't big on it with me. Obviously." I rolled my eyes. "We figure it was just a one-time attack anyway. The ... *thing*, whatever it was, will probably never come back."

"I'm not so sure about that," Tanner said, sneaking a glance at Hendrix, who now had his head down in his hands. Tanner grabbed my shoulder, leaning in, only a few inches away so that I stopped caring about whatever he was going to say and started wanting to drag him into the kitchen to have a little alone time until Anton showed up for the breakfast rush. That wasn't my proudest moment, but proximity with Tanner was intoxicating. Maybe someday soon I would get to perform a connection ritual with him. Mmm ...

"Forrest Uisce, that dryad that runs the farmland just west of Eastwind, I heard part of his crops were hit with an unexplained drought last night."

I hurried a step back. "For fang's sake. It's six fifteen in the morning! *How* has that gossip already reached you?"

Tanner looked confused. "The walk to work. I pass the Bouquets' house, Janet Timberhelm's apartment, Lance Flufferbum's shack, and Vic Hornsheart's lair."

"And they just, what, wait outside for you to pass and then tell you everything that's happened?"

Tanner shrugged defensively. "I don't think it's just me they wait for, but yeah, they fill me in when I pass."

I tried to wrap my mind around the organized gossip channels of this town. Didn't these people have anything better to do? "And how do they know?"

"Owls, Nora. Lots and lots of owls. But also Lance's brother, Lot Flufferbum, is the assistant chief editor at *The Eastwind Watch*, so he gets the scoop right when it happens. I wouldn't be surprised if he has spies around the city with the dirt he digs up, but that's another story entirely."

"One I'd like to hear *after* the one about Mr. and Mrs. Flufferbum naming their sons Lance and Lot. But okay." I shook my head to clear it. "What were we talking about?"

"Forrest. The drought at his farm."

"Right, right. That's not good." Tanner didn't realize, of course, that it was not good for a few reasons.

Predominantly, it meant I'd be seeing Donovan again after my shift. And we would be headed to the Deadwoods.

"Definitely not good," he replied. "Forrest is responsible for half of the nightshades in Eastwind. But also, it means there could be another attack."

"At least it's limited to plants," I said, trying to find the silver lining because, yes, I still felt slightly responsible for this happening, even though I knew I was myself a victim here.

"This town functions around plants, Nora. It's a

town run by witches. Witches need plants. Without plants, witches get cranky."

"They also get cranky when they're subjected to doom and gloom," I said, raising my eyebrows at him.

"What, me? I'm never doom and gloom."

I held up my hands in surrender. "Fine, you're right. I forgot who I was talking to. Tanner Culpepper is never doom and gloom. Or maybe you've been spending a little too much time around Grim."

"Or you," he said quickly.

I shrugged. "Fair enough. I need to freshen up before the breakfast rush hits. Would you mind getting that last table for me?"

His eyes went wide. "Are you trying to order me around, Nora Ashcroft?"

"Why not? I own half this place. Since you're the manager, technically that makes me your boss."

He laughed. "Not how that works, but sure. You do what you gotta do."

I strolled into the kitchen until I was out of Tanner's sight, then I jogged to the manager's office, jotted a note to Donovan that another attack had occurred and snuck out back to send it by owl.

* * *

By three p.m., with a half hour left in my shift, my nerves were getting the best of me. I knew I had to go into the Deadwoods to find what was there and hopefully stop it, but every time I gazed up from behind the counter, stared out the window, and found myself facing the edge of the forest, my stomach did a somersault.

I'd been in the Deadwoods only one time—back when I first arrived in Eastwind. I'd woken up there, disoriented after crossing over, and was totally unaware of the danger I was in, more interested in, first, following after the big, black dog who'd awoken me and, second, finding a telephone to call for a ride back to Austin.

Four and a half months later, and I still hadn't found a telephone, but since that day, I'd learned enough about the Deadwoods to know how lucky I'd been that I ever made it out. And now I was going to waltz right back in there. On purpose. Looking for trouble.

Tanner wasn't wrong about me. I was a magnet for trouble. And it was a magnet for me. I decided not to hold it against him that he'd made comments in a similar vein to his best friend.

Going over my possible suspects, yet again, was as unhelpful as it had been the first thirty-nine times. It was a not-seeing-the-forest-for-the-trees thing, I think, just like when I'd speak with the ghost of a murdered Eastwinder and their list of suspects was usually far from exhaustive. Oftentimes, the ones who wished the most harm on a person were especially talented at keeping that secret wish hidden from the intended victim.

My suspect list was weak, to be sure, and contingent upon the assumption that whoever had conjured the thing that knocked on Ruby's front door had both sent it there intentionally and was targeting me, rather than Ruby or Grim or Clifford. Those were some big assumptions, though. For one, Grim's tendency to mark his territory where he wasn't supposed to could easily earn him a few enemies. While he was my familiar, I certainly didn't keep track of him all the time, and his routine of showing up at Medium Rare hours after the start of my shift each day bought him a daily window of opportunity to stir up all kinds of trouble.

While I wasn't aware of any enemies Ruby might have, she'd certainly been in Eastwind long enough to earn some. From what I could tell, she wasn't besties with the Coven, but would they send an evil entity after her? That seemed unlikely, seeing as how obsessed they were with rules and order.

Perhaps only to make matters easier on myself, I'd ruled out Clifford as the intended target because he didn't do much of anything, and if I were going to eliminate one of us from the mix, he was the obvious choice.

That left me. Who were my enemies? Tandy Erixon and Frankie Jericho, obviously, since I'd played the lead role in getting each arrested for murder. But they were locked away in Ironhelm Penitentiary now, and from what I'd learned of the place, the structure had been fortified with layers and layers of powerful enchantments preventing any of the inmates from using magic. Presumably that included conjuring a demonic entity.

Could Tandy and Frankie have loved ones on the outside seeking revenge against me? It was entirely possible. I had never spoken to Frankie's husband, Heath Jericho. On the one hand, it had been his beloved sister who was murdered. On the other hand, his wife was now in prison for life, thanks to me. Whose side did he take in the matter? I had no clue.

Then there were the petty reasons for sending an entity after someone. Perhaps Seamus Shaw was upset that I rebuked him at Sheehan's and wanted to get even. I wasn't sure what level of magic leprechauns possessed, but he could have just as easily hired someone to conduct the conjuring. From what I heard, he came from money. Or maybe Sebastian Malavic wanted to send me a message to put me in my place. I wasn't sure why a vampire would need to bring something scarier than himself into the equation, but hey, I wasn't sure about a lot of things.

My list of suspects went on like that, one unlikely candidate after the next, each built on the two major assumptions that the attack was targeted and I was the intended target.

I had to drop it or I would give myself a migraine going in the same fruitless circle again and again. Instead, it made sense to focus on finding a solution to the problem at hand, and maybe in the process I would also stumble upon who was behind it.

In short, I needed to stop framing it as a whodunnit and start viewing it as a how-do-I-undo-it?

"You're here early," I said as Jane appeared from the back, coming to stand by me behind the counter as I started in on some of my side work after the tail end of the lunch rush. It wasn't until she was right next to me that I noticed the bags under her eyes. "Rough night?"

Slowly, she turned her head toward me, and it was clear I'd asked the wrong question. "I hope to the almighty goddess that you never have to spend a night with an angry and confused werebear."

"Um. Yeah, me too. What happened?"

She shook her head, pressing her palms into her eye sockets. "Looks like drought hit Whirligig's Garden Center late last night. Thaddeus is trying to keep it quiet so it doesn't hurt business, but Ansel is furious. He near about lost an eye while potting a belligerent totem pole cactus a few weeks back, and now the thing's two inches from death's doorstep and he's not sure it'll recover."

I swallowed hard. "The cacti were affected?"

She removed her hands from her eyes and turned to lean her side against the counter so she faced me head on. "Yeah, Nora. Strange, isn't it?" The controlled tone of her voice indicated that she did not find it all that strange. Ansel must have done what he said he would and told her about my visit two days before. "It was almost like the water was sucked right out of them."

"Fangs and claws," I cursed. "I'm so sorry."

"Why should you be sorry?" she said, one of her dark brows levitating high above her light-brown eyes. "You didn't kill the cactus, right? Just like you didn't also drink half the water in Glacier Lake."

"Glacier Lake?" I asked. "Up on Fluke Mountain?"

She nodded slowly as a yawn overtook her. "Yep. Darius is losing it, too."

"Wait, who's Darius again?"

"Darius Pine. The love of Ansel's life. Their bromance would make me jealous, except I'd feel smothered if Ansel ever looked at me the way he does Darius. Maybe it's just a werebear thing. Darius is head of Ansel's clan, actually, and owns the cabins and lumberyard up on Fluke Mountain. He's also the one I was going to set you up with until I realized you were unavailable."

"I don't know what you're—"

Her hand shot into the air between us. "Save it. I don't have the patience for lies this morning."

"I'm sorry, Jane. If it makes you feel any better, I'm doing what I can to get the drought issue sorted. Donovan and I are—"

"Donovan?" She chuckled. "You managed to rope Mr. Not My Problem into this? Wow, Nora, I'm impressed. Especially with the way he feels about you." She stood up straight and inhaled through her nose. On the exhale, she said, "Okay," then nodded. "I see you mean business getting this figured out, so I'll save all the grief I was going to give you for something else that you inevitably stir up."

"You're so merciful," I grumbled.

"Never been called that before." She patted me on the shoulder. "Enjoy your side work. I'm going to chug a pot of coffee in the back." I thought she was kidding until she grabbed a full pot from the cradle on the counter next to me and took it with her into the kitchen.

I put in an order to-go—two sunrise burgers and loaded fries—so that it would be ready by the time my shift was over. I figured if I was going to drag Donovan into the Deadwoods with me, endangering his life or whatnot, I ought to bring him something to eat first.

And maybe I was hoping to butter him up. After all, he was the witch who would have my back in this, and the more incentive I could provide for him to do a bang-up job of it, the better.

It didn't occur to me until I saw him enter, sweat stains under his arms visible from yards away, that Deputy Stu Manchester hadn't made it in for breakfast this morning. I prided myself on keeping tabs of the regulars, but my mind had been somewhere else all morning (specifically, standing at the edge of a dark tunnel of trees), and I'd forgotten to double-check my mental manifest. I hurried to get the coffee and pie served up for him before he made it to the countertop.

Man, he looked rough this afternoon. The odds were good that he'd been awake nearly twenty-four hours, if he was coming in at this time. Something had held him over, and I was almost afraid to ask.

The pie and coffee were there for him as he slid onto the stool, and an ice water followed shortly after.

"You gonna make it today, Deputy?" I asked.

"It'd be a miracle if I did, Ms. Ashcroft." He downed the entire glass of water and proceeded to chew the ice before I came over with a pitcher to refill. "Thank you. Never been thirstier after a day on the job."

"It's hot out there, that's for sure."

He waved me off and stuck the first bite of cherry pie into his mouth. "Nah, not the heat. The drought! Plus the fighting. Plus the ... well, the everything."

Oh boy.

"This sounds suspiciously like something you might have played a part in," said Grim from the spot below the counter where he'd taken up residence a few hours before.

"We don't know that."

"I'd put money on it, if I had some. Would you put money on it?"

"Sure."

"Great. Let's put money on it."

"Um, not right now. You just said you don't have money anyway."

"Doesn't matter if I have money or not. You'll be the one paying up. Guarantee it."

"*No deal.*"

"Want to talk about it?" I asked Deputy Manchester. "You know I'm good for it."

He looked up at me, head still tilted downward toward his pie, then exhaled. "Actually, yes. I could use an ear."

I smiled and nodded for him to go ahead.

He sighed, sat up straight, adjusting his duty belt, and stared vaguely at the ceiling. "Where do I begin? Okay, how about the fact that if I see another leprechaun today, I'm going to quit this job once and for all, and Eastwind can learn to clean up its own messes?"

After a quick scan of the restaurant to make sure we didn't have any leprechauns present, which we did not, I asked, "What happened with the leprechauns?"

"For fang's sake, what *didn't* happen with the leprechauns is the easier question to answer." He grabbed a napkin and rubbed it over his forehead, soaking up sweat and grime. "Erin Park is a complete disaster. First, I get word that all the booze at Sheehan's Pub is gone—of course they'd notice *that* first."

"*Huh,*" said Grim. "*Sounds a lot like what happened with Ruby's tea.*"

I ignored him.

Stu continued venting. "I'm already trying to single-handedly prevent that entire neighborhood from rioting once word gets around, which takes, oh, half an hour, then an emergency owl swoops in to inform me that Rainbow Falls has slowed to a trickle!"

"*Oh boy,*" Grim said quickly.

"*What? Why 'oh boy'?*"

"*You don't know about Rainbow Falls?*"

"No. Should I? I'm not a leprechaun. I almost never go over to Erin Park."

"Well," said Stu, "you can imagine the worst-case scenario there."

"Totally," I lied. "And did it come to pass?"

His head swiveled quickly, checking his surroundings before he leaned over the counter. I leaned over, too, since he obviously wanted the next bit to remain between us. "Yes." He stared at me wide-eyed, and I suspected I was supposed to be following along.

"Rainbow Falls protects the town's gold reserves," Grim supplied in uncharacteristically helpful fashion. *"They're stored in a cave behind it. No one can get past the falls except the Guardian ... unless the falls dry up, then—*

"Oh, holy shifter."

"The gold is gone?" I spat. Cringing, I looked around. Only Ted seemed to be paying attention to me, but that was sort of a given. "Sorry," I whispered.

"It's true." He nodded, his shoulders slumped, and he shoved nearly half the pie into his mouth in a single heaping forkful.

"The gold is gone," I repeated dumbly.

Through a stuffed mouth, he replied, "Well, not gone. I mean, it's *somewhere*. Probably. Assuming none of you lot vanished it with a flick of your wand. Don't know why anyone in their right mind would do that, but there are plenty of witches *not* in their right mind. I'm gonna need another piece of pie," he added.

Now that he'd gotten the worst bit of news off his chest, he appeared much less burdened, sitting up straight, rolling his shoulders to loosen them. "Yep," he said around another mouthful of cherries and crust, "this town will burn itself to the ground when word gets out in approximately twenty-three minutes and eighteen seconds." He sucked in coffee and mashed it around with the pie. "Oh, and on top of it all, Whirligig's Garden Center and Forrest Uisce's farm suffered losses that they're attributing to magic. And you know what?" He cackled. "I don't even have time to care! Because the leprechauns! With their pointy shoes and thinly veiled alcoholism and death threats! Ha! This town is going to fold in on itself in a matter of days, and *then* who's going to be in support of budget cuts to keep from hiring more deputies? Not even Mayor Esperia is going to raise a stink about it now!" He chugged his coffee, wincing against the heat, no doubt, before raising the mug up to me. "Keep it coming."

"Special delivery," said Tanner from behind me. He carried two to-go boxes with a folded and sealed letter on top. "Somebody's hungry," he said, handing over the boxes.

I smiled but didn't reply.

"And this letter just came for you."

"Thanks," I said. "Could you get Deputy Manchester a refill while I see what this is about?"

"Of course." He turned to Deputy Manchester. "You're in awfully late in the day, Stu."

I cleared my throat until Tanner looked, then I shook my head quickly, mouthing, *Don't ask.*

"I, uh, let me get you that coffee." Tanner scooted away and I pulled open the sealed letter. It just said, *Fine. Come over. Bring food. Don't tell T.*

I crumpled it up and stuck it in my apron just as

Tanner snuck up behind me. "Anything good?" he said playfully.

"Nah, nothing. Just Ruby. She wanted to know if I would stop by the butcher's on the way back."

"Ah, is that burger for her then?"

"Nope."

His eyes narrowed almost imperceptibly. "O-kay. Not feeling talkative. Fair enough. It's been a crazy shift. Hey, I was wondering if you wanted to come over tonight and we can try the flavor enhancer potion again. This time *without* letting Monster screw it up with one of her hairballs. Not looking to switch bodies with Grim again."

I wasn't in a hurry for a repeat, either. Hearing Grim's words come from Tanner's mouth was certified nightmare material. Almost turned me off of potion practice for good. "I'd love to. But, um, I have plans tonight." I grimaced apologetically. "Maybe tomorrow?"

"Who do you have plans with?" he asked, the words tumbling headfirst from him.

"Donovan." I cringed my apology.

Tanner's mouth popped open, and his eyebrows pinched together. "Oh. Okay." He paused. "Can I come?"

Oof. "Uh, we were just going to address the issue of" —Stu didn't seem to be listening, but no point risking it— "you know, since it seems like it *wasn't* a one-time thing." My mind searched for a good excuse until it landed on a fairly strong one, if I do say so myself. I moved closer to him and set my hands on his hips just below the level of the countertop. Sliding my palms just a little farther toward the back, I murmured, "I won't be there long, and

I'm afraid if you come, I'll be too distracted and we won't make any progress."

As color filled his cheeks and his gaze darted to the customers closest to us who were most likely to catch a glimpse of what was going on behind the counter, a smile turned a single corner of his lips, and I knew my excuse was an effective one. "Yeah, okay. I wouldn't want that. We can work on it tomorrow. Jane looks like she was sat on by a dragon-shifter, so I'll send her home and cover for her tonight."

"Do you ever sleep, Tanner Culpepper?"

He laughed and stepped away from me. "Only when I'm tired."

I untied my apron, folding it and wrapping the strings around the middle. "You must have endless energy, then."

As he walked past me, he leaned close and mumbled, "Endless stamina, too."

My jaw fell open, as he walked casually as ever toward a table full of fairies who'd just sat down. "Don't forget the burgers for you and Donovan," he called over his shoulder. "Good luck."

Chapter Nine

Donovan popped the last lukewarm cheese fry in his mouth. As I'd suspected I would, I regretted letting Grim eat all my loaded fries on the walk over from Medium Rare.

Neither Donovan nor I spoke while we ate at his low living room table, and I assumed that was because neither of us wanted to. Not while there was a sunrise burger getting cold and, oh yeah, we didn't really like each other.

He took our empty boxes to be composted and returned a moment later with a heavy tome bound in cracked black leather, and a small cauldron. "I have an idea," he said.

"Great, I'm all for ideas."

"I found a spell that I think will help focus the channeling so we can ask specific questions and get answers."

"Oh wow. Sounds perfect. Good work."

He glanced up from the book, no doubt making sure I wasn't being sarcastic. I wasn't.

Flipping open to the page, he pointed at the title.

"I don't know what that says," I admitted. It was in ancient runes. Or what I suspected was ancient runes based on my limited exposure to it over the past months.

I half expected him to say something like, "typical" or "when are you going to learn how to do basic things?" but he said nothing along those lines. It was as if his enthusiasm had stomped out his bitterness.

"It translates roughly to 'conjure quest.' I've never used it myself because it specifically requires a Fifth Wind witch to be present for it." He giggled excitedly. "Man, oh man. Probably no one alive in Eastwind today has tried it. I can't wait to see that know-it-all Oliver's face when I tell him I've gone on a conjure quest."

"Ah yes, *there's* the bitterness I know and love."

"Listen, you'd feel the same way if you had to sit in classes with him for years, watching him answer every question exactly by the books."

"You're probably right. So, what do we do for this conjure quest thing?"

He inhaled deeply, blowing it out in a whoosh. "Right. It's a complicated spell, and, fair warning, it requires blood."

I leaned back, my hands raised in surrender. "Nope. I'm out."

"Oh come on. Don't tell me you'll rush headfirst and blind into the Deadwoods but you're afraid of blood."

I shook my head. "It's not that at all. It's that Ruby has expressly forbid me from doing any spells that involve my blood until we've trained more. She says they could be more powerful than I can handle."

"She's absolutely right. Now, are you in or out?"

I thought about how haggard Deputy Manchester looked when he'd walked into the diner that afternoon. What had started as a simple annoyance was quickly spiraling out of control into a town crisis. Who knew what came next? "Fine. In."

A mischievous grin spread across his lips. "I thought so." He chuckled. "Tanner doesn't appreciate this side of you, you know. Not like he should."

"What side?" I said, taken aback by the sudden mention of Tanner.

"The reckless side. He wants you to stay safe. He might even be okay with it making you miserable in the long-term."

"Now you're just talking out of your a—"

"I like it, though," he said. "That is, as long as you don't get me killed. Oh, speaking of which, just so we're clear, if you do get me killed, I'm one hundred percent haunting you until the end of time."

"That's just uncalled for," I said. "I'm not going to get you killed. *You're* going to get you killed. For fang's sake, take a little personal responsibility for your own death."

He reached out from his place on a cushion right next to mine and grabbed my hand firmly. My gaze darted from where our hands touched to his face. What did he think he was doing?

Then he pulled his wand from his waistband. "This will only hurt a little bit."

"Are you going to do it, too?"

He rolled his eyes. "Of course. But you first, so I know you won't chicken out."

"I'm not going to chicken— *ouch!*"

A crack opened up along the pad of my thumb where

he'd touched his wand. As the blood began to collect, he lifted my hand over the tiny cauldron and squeezed my split skin, draining five drops of blood from it as I sucked in air against the pain.

Once he let go of my hand, I made to suck on my sore thumb, but his hand shot forward and pushed mine back down. "You don't want to do that," he said, his intense blue eyes boring into me underneath dark and serious eyebrows. "Here." He touched his wand to my thumb again, and the cut closed up, though the pain still smarted.

He added his blood to the cauldron next, followed by a few drops of the spring water from the center of the table.

"Is that it?" I asked.

"Almost." He looked past me to the dark corner where Grim had settled himself. "Grim, can you come here for a second?"

"Absolutely not."

"What do you need with Grim?" I asked.

"The spell calls for a toenail off a dead animal. So unless you want to go find a dead animal, or kill one yourself, Grim is our best option."

Grim growled low. *"Screw off. I've never felt more alive."*

"Come on, Grim. It's just a toenail. Yours have gotten frighteningly long lately anyway. They're making you walk funny."

"That's because I don't have twigs and sharp rocks breaking them off as I hunt in the woods. Now that I'm domesticated, it's your responsibility to trim them."

"Okay, that's not going to happen, but I can take you to Echo's Salon and have them do it."

"Talk about things that are not going to happen."

"Just come over here," I said. *"At least we'll have one down and ... how many more would you have left?"*

"You seriously don't know how many toes a dog has?"

"Does he not know his name?" Donovan suggested.

"He knows his name," I snapped back. "Grim. We're not going to the Deadwoods if you don't come over here."

With a laborious grunt, he lifted himself from the corner and lumbered over, begrudgingly offering his paw to Donovan. *"This guy probably knows all about preening."*

"Are you seriously stereotyping him because you still think he's gay?"

"No, I'm stereotyping him because his house is immaculate and he's dreamy and smells nice."

Grim was right on all counts. Well, not the dreamy part. Nope. I mean, maybe if he weren't such a jerk to me and lightened up a little bit. Sure, then I could see how some *other* girl might find him dreamy. Especially with those piercing eyes, that full head of messy mocha hair that begged for fingers to run through it ...

"Okay, all done," he said.

"Huh?"

Grim retreated to his corner again.

"We're ready for the conjure quest. Oh, wait. One more thing." His eyes fell to my chest. "You'll need to take it off."

No. He couldn't be telling me to undress in front of him. Did he really think I'd fall for that? Human or witch —men were all the same when it came down to it, and I'd seen enough in my time not to naively take the bait. "Not a chance."

He sighed exasperatedly. "Nora, there's no way this will work while you're wearing that."

"Unicorn swirls," I spat. "It worked last time just fine."

"Nooo ..." he said, side-eying me like I was crazy. "You took it off last time. It's designed to keep you from channeling, Nora. You have to take it off if you—"

"Ohh! The amulet? You mean the amulet."

His wide eyes made him resemble a spooked horse. "Yes. What did you think I meant? Did you think I was trying to get you to—"

I waved him off, shaking my head. "Nothing, nothing. Just a little slow after the burger." I reached down the front of my shirt and grabbed the staurolite amulet. "Let's never speak of this again, please."

"Um, sure."

Once I'd set it aside, he placed the cauldron on the ground between us, wet his hands and indicated I should do the same. We clasped hands firmly then, and he said, "You're going to have to take the lead here, since you're the wind responsible for channeling. Think of three questions you want answered, and be sure to only ask one at a time."

"Do I ask it aloud?"

"No, just in your mind."

"Okay. I have them."

"Now we need to time our breathing. Breathe in when I squeeze your hands, breathe out when I release. Once we're in sync, I'll begin the incantation."

I let my mind relax, focusing only on Donovan's hand

grasping mine and the feel my chest rising and falling. Before long, we breathed together, long, deep inhales and slow exhales. The energy cycled between us, and I started to lose track of where my body ended and his began as the circle strengthened. And as he muttered the incantation, I felt it all around me. Through me. Then I focused on my first question.

What is the entity causing this damage around Eastwind?

The darkness behind my eyelids lit up, scenery blowing by me as I rushed forward. Only, I wasn't me. I was the thing again.

It cut through town, up the cobblestone streets, past stores I frequented, arriving at the ivy-covered stone archway into the garden center. It didn't stop there, though, blowing past in the pre-dawn darkness, and soaring over the rows of sleepy and lethargic cacti. A high pitch squeal rose up from the plants, and I knew what was happening beneath.

And then I could see it. I was outside of the thing, Donovan standing next to me. The dark entity circled over the plants, sucking water vapor up into itself like steam disappearing into a black hole.

I could almost make out a form, too. While the back half was nebulous, swirling like a thick black smoke, the front resembled the body of a woman, her arms outstretched ahead of her, grasping at air as she soared.

I recentered my mind on my question. *What is the entity causing this damage around Eastwind?* Then we were standing in a strange field. The greenery seemed like something out of Erin Park, only it was another place. Somewhere entirely different and not of this world. I was sure of that. On the far end of the flat space loomed a giant wall of impenetrable jungle.

And then the soldiers appeared.

Two armies facing off, a two-hundred-yard stretch of green the only thing separating them as they marched toward each other. One side dressed in bloodred armor had nearly double the manpower. But the other side, wearing a hodgepodge of grays and browns, had its own special weapons.

Floating just ahead of the front line of the outmanned army were two massive floating figures, one white and wispy as a cloud, the other deep blue with a form that wobbled slightly. They hovered in place until the head of the small army shouted. Then the blue being rushed forward against the oncoming forces. The sky darkened as clouds formed above the red army, swirling, thickening, until the storm broke. The ragtag army remained dry, unaffected by the rain.

The blue form danced in the sky, and as its movements whipped faster, the intensity of the storm pummeled the advancing red army. It slowed them, blurred their vision, but it didn't stop them.

Then the wispy white figure took its place beside the blue and began a dance of its own, and as it did, I had to grab onto Donovan to keep from being blown off my feet by the conjured squalls. Then the winds changed, hitting the red army headlong, preventing each of their steps forward from yielding any progress.

Until one of the men of the red army, crawling on his hands and knees, his uniform more detailed and ornate than the others', managed to separate himself from the back. He drove a longsword into the earth to keep from blowing away as he knelt and bowed his head.

A shriek pierced the sky, causing both the white and blue entities to pause in their dance. The rain stopped. The winds calmed. Both armies stood frozen, as did Donovan and I, looking around for the source of the horrific sound.

There it was, tearing out of the jungle, cutting through the air like a rocket. The black entity. And below it, the green fields shriveled, their water vaporizing and disappearing into the mass, just like at the garden center.

It immediately engaged the blue and white beings, and the three fought in a midair swirl of fury while below the armies charged. So caught up in the scene unfolding ahead of me, I almost didn't hear Donovan shout for me to ask the next question. Already? But I wanted to see how this battle played out.

He was right, though. I could feel it. I'd seen all I was meant to see here. So I asked the next question.

Who summoned that entity to Eastwind?

With a wave of vertigo, I was transported to the Outskirts, the Deadwoods only fifty yards behind me as I stared ahead at Medium Rare, the early afternoon sun glaring overhead. What day was it?

The door burst open and at first, I couldn't make out who was leaving—the image was blurry. I went through my list of suspects. Was it Seamus? Or Sebastian? Or maybe someone else entirely who I didn't even knew held a grudge against me? Either way, I felt like whoever this was, he or she was also the answer to my second question.

Then two figures emerged, heading toward us, one

taller with dark hair, the other short and round with strawberry-blond curls.

"No," I breathed. "Those numbskulls? Really? It couldn't be them."

They came within feet of where we stood, but didn't spare us a glance. "Stupid stuck-up witch," mumbled the dark-haired boy. "Thinks she's hot stuff because she can yell at us in public. Of course everyone will take her side. They always take the woman's side."

"You shouldn't have done that, Duncan," muttered the short one. "If Mancer hears about that, we could be suspended. You know how they get about harassing elder witches."

"Please, she's not an elder witch. Way I heard it, she's not even a real witch. Just some death-obsessed wannabe." He punched his friend. "What's with you, Tybalt? You let a woman humiliate you in front of everyone and you just roll over and take it? I didn't know you were such a pixie."

"I'm not a pixie!" demanded Tybalt. "You're a pixie!" He punched Duncan in the arm.

Duncan snarled. "They're all going to think we're a couple of pixies if we don't do anything about it."

Tybalt rolled his eyes. "What could we do about it? We're not even allowed to use wands yet."

"Not allowed and not able are two different things. I have an idea. Follow me."

They ran off down the street toward Fulcrum Park, and when I wasn't able to follow, I knew it was time for my final question.

How do we stop it?

Our surroundings went dark around us, all except for

an object hovering a few feet off the ground twenty or so yards ahead. I took a step forward, and Donovan's arm bolted out, blocking my way.

"It won't hurt me," I said.

"You don't know that. Just be careful."

He lowered his arm but followed his advice, approaching with caution. Light radiated around it, and once I was within feet of it and realized what it was, I almost laughed. "It's just a book."

"You say that like books can't kill you."

I arched a brow. "I wasn't aware of that danger, no."

"Well, they can."

"Great. Add it to the list of things in this town that can kill me." I leaned over the book without making contact and tried to read the cover. It was worn and brown, and I only detected glimpses of gold lettering that might've once reflected boldly, spelling out what in the world I was looking at. "I think the answer is in this book."

"That's a safe bet."

Okay, so if the answer to my question was in the book, what was I waiting for? I pushed aside my newfound bibliophobia, and grasped the cover.

As soon as I did, the book disappeared, and we stood at the entrance of the tree tunnel again.

"For fang's sake," I said. "Not this again."

Then my stomach did a flip. I was falling. I was falling straight down into nothingness, and Donovan was falling beside me.

And then I hit the ground. I was back in Donovan's living room.

And lying facedown on top of him.

I groaned but couldn't yet move as the world spun around me. "I'm gonna vomit," I moaned.

"Please get off of me before you do."

"I don't know if I can."

"Ugh," he moaned. "I think I might vomit, too."

And just like that, I found the strength to roll off of him.

We lay on our backs, panting, regaining control of our stomachs like the adults we were.

Finally, Donovan broke the silence. "Duncan and Tybalt. Were they talking about you?"

"I think so."

With a groaning effort, he rolled onto his side to face me, propping up onto his elbow. "What happened?"

I turned my head, staring up at his pained face, thinking, *Please don't vomit on me.*

"The short one, Tybalt. He was harassing me a little bit. I was going to ignore it, but when I turned around, Duncan pinched my butt."

Donovan's eyes narrowed and his top lip curled in disgust. "Are you serious?"

"Yeah, I know, who would want to pinch my butt, right?"

"No, that's not— So then what happened?"

"I kicked them out. I told them they needed to leave, and when they refused, I, um, might've made a scene." I grimaced apologetically. "Maybe if I hadn't made a scene solely to humiliate them, they wouldn't have felt compelled to retaliate. That *is* what you gathered from the vision, right?"

"More or less. But let's back up to the part where you

blame yourself for teaching a couple of screw-up teenage boys a lesson. This is *not* your fault, Nora."

My stomach was finally settled, and I sat up. "I'm sure I could have handled it better."

"Oh wait, did you slap them so hard their astral forms flew out of their ears?"

I laughed. "No."

"Mm-hm," he said, pressing his lips together and nodding knowingly. "See, that's what I would've done in your position. So I think you handled it about as good as anyone could." His expression softened as he sat up to face me. "Seriously, Nora, do not blame yourself. I've seen those little witches around town. They're constant trouble. Honestly, it's a miracle they haven't gotten themselves killed, messing around like they do. And if no one puts them in their place now, they're just going to become older and stronger bullies. You did the right thing."

"Thanks," I said, feeling off-balance, though whether that was a remnant from the out-of-body experience or because Donovan had just been uncharacteristically supportive, I wasn't sure. "It doesn't change the fact that there's a whatever-the-spell dark entity running around, and we don't know all that much about it." I sighed. "I guess I dropped the ball on the questions, because I don't feel like we have the answers we need."

"Don't be stupid," he said, and the bluntness of it was comforting. This was the Donovan I knew. "We got plenty of information from the vision. We have a good idea of who summoned the thing, let's call it a demon, and I'm pretty sure the answer to how we banish it is in a book."

"Awesome. Because there aren't enough books to fill a coliseum scattered around this town," I said impatiently. "Are we just supposed to go door to door asking people if we can browse their bookshelves?"

"Riiight," he said, inspecting me closely. "You don't know."

"I don't know what?"

"Every book brought into Eastwind has an identical copy magically appear in the appropriate section of the Eastwind Library. If the book exists in this world, we can find it there."

That was pretty freaking cool. And no, I didn't know that. Someone seriously needed to write a guidebook for this place. "Only one problem," I said. "We don't know what it's called or what it's about. We only know what it looks like. And even *I* can name three other books I've seen that look almost identical to that one."

"Sweet baby jackalope," he spat. "For someone who likes running head-on into tricky situations, you sure construct a lot of obstacles between you and the easy stuff." He stood, taking the spell book and cauldron with him.

I wasn't going to let him drop a bomb like that and walk away, though, so I followed him into his kitchen, where he set the items on the marble counter. "What do you mean?"

He lit a candle and held the cauldron over the flame. "I mean exactly what I said. You'll lure a murderous xana into your home or follow an equally murderous nix to a dark storeroom, no sweat. I mean, holy shifter, you were willing to charge into the Deadwoods with nothing but your unhelpful familiar as backup. But when it comes to going into a library in search of a book you need or, oh, I don't know, going public with your relationship, you can't bring yourself to go there."

"Why do you care about *that*?" I said.

"I don't." He poured the smoking contents of the cauldron into a bowl of water, then set it back down on the counter before grabbing the book and walking away.

I pursued him into a narrow hallway lined with books. "You do care, or else you wouldn't have brought it up."

"I just think it's peculiar." He turned quickly, and I had to catch myself before I ran straight into him. He stepped closer, and I tried to move away, but my back found a bookshelf. I was pinned, and my heart raced.

"It's not that peculiar," I countered.

His warm breath caressed my face as he spoke. "I guess not. After all, I'm the exact same."

He placed the book back on the shelf just above my right shoulder then made for the kitchen again. "You coming with me to the big, bad library, or what?" he hollered.

"Yes," I said, my voice cracking. I cleared my throat, my back still against the shelf as I tried to slow my fluttering heart. Then I repeated, making sure my voice didn't waver this time. "Yes, I'm coming."

Chapter Ten

"I'm surprised you don't spend all your free-time here, to be honest," Donovan said as we crossed the bright, open entry hall of the library, carefully avoiding the books that floated this way and that. "If I was a Fifth Wind witch, I would spend all day here, picking the brain of every ghost who would spare me the time."

"Nerd," said Grim.

"You say that," I replied, "but only because you haven't spent the past four months being pestered by them." Spirits bustled around us, lining the long studying tables, hunched as they pored over books. Some enchantment existed at the library that allowed ghosts to move things without effort, a skill usually reserved for poltergeist, or so I'd been told. But here, they were able to select the book they chose from the shelf, carry it around, and even turn individual pages. It wasn't the worst way to while away the hours stuck between astral planes. "If there's one thing I know about ghosts," I continued, "it's that they all want something. And they won't stop until they get it."

Donovan narrowly avoided taking a book to the groin with a quick side step. "And that's different from you and me ... how?"

I laughed. "I *wish* I knew what I wanted."

"You don't? You strike me as the kind of woman knows exactly what she wants. Or who."

I shot him a nasty look. "We're not talking about that. And what about you, Mr. Career Bartender. Are you telling me you know exactly what you want?"

"Absolutely."

I stopped in my tracks. "And that is?"

He shrugged. "To be left in peace, mostly." He started forward again, and I hurried to keep up. "And see? I'm doing whatever it takes to achieve that."

"How so?"

"I'm risking my hide by going into the Deadwoods with you because I know seeing this thing through will allow me peace in one of two ways: either we solve it and banish this demon thing so you and Tanner can go on your appallingly merry way with life and I can go back to my pleasant routine, or you get me killed, and I can rest in peace for all eternity."

"I thought you said you would haunt me if this got you killed."

"Right," he said. "I mean, *after* I haunted you for the rest of your life, I would rest in peace. After all, when compared with eternity, the rest of your life is less than a blink of an eye."

"*He has a point,*" Grim said from behind me.

Donovan led the way to the tall reference desk,

leaning his elbows on the top and grinning wide at Helena Whetstone, the elf librarian who was likely older than most of the ghosts she spent her days around. She appeared, like most elves, to be much, much younger than her age. I would have guessed mid-forties, but who only knew what that was in elf years.

"Helena," he said. "How're you this evening?"

She looked up from where she was working on some sort of numbers puzzle that I can only describe as Sudoku if the boxes constantly leap-frogged over each other. "Yes, Mr. Stringfellow? What do you want now?"

Customer service at its finest, I tell you.

"We're looking for a book."

She frowned. "Ah, I can't help you, then. Fresh out of books." She looked back down at the puzzle.

A muscle in Donovan's jaw tightened, and I wondered if he knew how much enjoyment I was getting out of this.

"It's old, brown cover, might have something about an ancient dark entity?"

Pursing her lips, Helena returned her attention to Donovan. "You're going to have to do better than that."

"That's all I know about it."

"Then you should learn more about it and come back. We're open every day, six a.m. to midnight." She cleared her throat and smacked her hand down on the puzzle to keep one of the squares from running off the page.

"Could you at least—"

She stuck her hand an inch from his nose, and he straightened quickly. "No. Not until you have a more specific title, author, or subject matter. Sorry."

A vein in Donovan's forehead bulged as he wisely put a little distance between him and Helena.

"Maybe someone else here knows," I suggested.

He looked around. "Who, Anton?" He nodded over at the ogre cook from Medium Rare, who spent most of his free time reading anything he could get his club-like hands on.

"Maybe," I said. "He practically lives here." I paused. "Actually, he *might* live here." I waved it off. "Doesn't matter. Wouldn't hurt to ask him about the book."

"You sure?" Donovan said, staring cautiously at him.

"Please," I said, approaching the ogre, "Anton wouldn't hurt a fly."

I forewent mentioning that I'd once seen him snatch a fly out of the air and proceed to eat it. In his defense, it would've otherwise landed on the food he was cooking, and that was unsanitary.

No, eating it wouldn't have been my first choice, either, but I try not to nitpick how people, especially ogres, choose to live their lives.

"Anton," I whispered as we neared.

He gazed up, his eyes slightly crossed toward his massive, pore-riddled nose. "Nora?"

He seemed a bit dazed. Almost felt bad interrupting the guy. He'd worked a crazy shift this morning and deserved his alone time to unwind. "Hey, I have a question you might be able to help me with."

Anton grunted, as per usual.

"I'm looking for a book and Helena isn't being especially helpful."

He grunted again, and I assumed it was ogre for, "What's new?"

"It's about this thick"—I indicated with my thumb and pointer—"brown, has illegible gold lettering, and contains information about a dark entity who can suck water from plants."

He blinked slowly, then his focus shifted to Donovan. "He's with me," I explained. "Can you help us?"

Grunting again, Anton rocked himself sideways out of the chair and to his feet. He was built like a retired boxer with a lingering steroid addiction, and Donovan took a half-step back when the ogre began swinging his arms side to side. But Anton was simply stretching his back.

"Follow," he rumbled, so we did.

We passed under a dark stone archway into a claustrophobic hallway leading into another wing of the library. Turning one corner after the next, taking a left at this Y and a right at another, sloping steadily downward until I wasn't sure we were still in Eastwind, the room we eventually entered wasn't much more spacious than the hallway had been. A single reading table was visible at the far end of a space that resembled a wine cellar more than a library. The walls were faded stone, and I was sure the temperature had dropped at least fifteen degrees from when we left the main gallery. Rows of books fanned out on either side of the table, chains dangling loosely, securing assorted tomes to their shelf.

And at the table sat a single lonely spirit. With the body of a man and the head of a bull, he was not someone I wanted to strike up a conversation with. Then it occurred to me: Anton had just pointed straight at a ghost. "Wait, can you see him?"

His grunt sounded suspiciously like "duh."

"And he might know about the book?"

Anton grunted again, turned, and left.

"I hate to doubt Anton's legendary friendship," said Grim, *"but did he just lead us all this way to be killed? Are we a sacrifice for that thing?"*

"I wish I could tell you. We'll find out soon enough."

"Do you see something?" Donovan asked, scanning the room blankly. "I mean, besides the books that are radiating alarming energy?"

"Yeah. There's someone at the table."

When the beastly spirit turned a page of the book he had engrossed himself in, Donovan nodded. "Ah. Okay." Then he mumbled, "This seems like your type of thing—super dangerous, going in blind, et cetera. Lead the way."

Maybe Donovan had a point after all, because approaching this strange spirit with horns that, in life, could probably gore someone as thick as Anton, didn't worry me. Or rather, it did, but my brain was able to compartmentalize it fairly quickly. Especially after I reached down and felt the amulet beneath my shirt. "Excuse me," I said.

The ghost's head snapped up quickly, and a puff of steam issued from his snout. His dark eyes observed us carefully before he replied, "Which book?"

"It's about this thick—"

"Stop." His voice was thick with finality. "Don't tell me about it. Show me." He held out his hand, a human hand, thank Gaia, because for some reason, a ghost hoof would have been too much. I approached the table, paused, looked back, and saw that neither Grim nor Donovan was following behind.

"Some back-up you are, Grim."

"I said I'd follow you into the Deadwoods. Bullhead over here wasn't part of the plan."

"The library was, though."

"You expect me to anticipate that a quick trip to the library equals a heart-to-heart with a minotaur's spirit?"

"Is that what he is?"

"You—" Grim shook his fluffy head. *"You don't even know what he is, and you're about to take his hand? Sweet baby jackalope, some people just can't be helped."*

Did it matter that he used to be a minotaur? Now, his primary form was spirit. And I knew a little about spirits. Not much. But more than I knew about minotaurs, that's for sure.

Despite Grim's disappointment in me, I reached out and took the minotaur's icy hand. It felt solid, not like the other ghosts I'd encountered, and my heart raced. Was this a different kind of spirit than I was used to?

I quickly discovered this wasn't even *close* to the kind of spirit I was used to.

"Close your eyes," he said, so I did. "Conjure the book in your mind."

Steadying my breathing, I let the image of the book floating in the darkness surface in my mind's eye.

Then, next to it, the minotaur appeared in full, living form. He reached forward, grabbed the book out of the air, and turned it over in his hands, examining every inch. "More," he said, and it felt like he spoke to me from my memory rather than the room in which we stood.

"More?" I said. "More what?"

"You know," he replied. "Relax and let it out."

I did, and the battlefield reappeared. Only, the battle was over. Bodies were strewn everywhere, limp, baking in the sun. The shock of it must have caused me to tense, and I found myself back in the cold chamber of the Eastwind Library. I released his hand immediately, staring wide-eyed at him.

"That book hasn't been read in many years. What is your intent?"

"To send it back," I said quickly.

He bowed his head. "Then follow me, Nora."

While I hadn't provided my name, I wasn't surprised he knew it. After all, he'd just seen inside my head. Who knew what sort of dirt he had on me. Incredibly unsettling to consider, but at the same time, he probably encountered two beings who could communicate with him per decade, and he didn't strike me as the gossiping type.

However, it didn't seem right that he should know my name while I hadn't made an effort to learn his, so I asked, "What's your name?" fully intending to use it as often as possible henceforth to butter him up just a bit. Couldn't hurt to have a minotaur warm up to you, right?

"No name. Not anymore."

O-kay then.

The book he led me to was connected to the bookshelves by a heavy iron chain a few feet long which clanked as he pulled the tome from its spot and offered it to me. I was almost afraid to touch it, but when he shoved it toward me, I reacted, and I was touching it before I knew what had happened.

Gazing down at it, I knew this was the one. Not just because of the brown cover and faded gold lettering, but because the image of the battlefield, before the carnage took place, became almost as vivid to my eyes as my physical surroundings.

"That's it," said Donovan, hovering over my shoulder. "That's the book."

"No kidding," I said.

As I opened the book to the first page, I didn't know what to expect. Latin? Chinese? Sanskrit? When the words were in English, I was pleasantly surprised. The title page said *Origins of the Unnatural, Vol. 394, Omzarka-Ostrogalia.*

While the table of contents was also in English, it was full of words I'd never seen before. The chapters were in alphabetical order, but that was all the sense I could make of it.

"Omzarka, Onanchant, Onasias?" I looked up at the minotaur. "Am I supposed to know what any of this means?"

"Wait," said Donovan behind me. He leaned forward, and pointed to one of the words. "Oquay. I know about that. It's one of the realms directly connected to Avalon."

"One of the realms?"

"Yeah. Avalon is a central realm—some refer to it as a pivot world—and it has a bunch of other realms branching off from it through various gateways. Like, hundreds. I don't know them all, but I do know Oquay is one of them."

"Is Eastwind one of them, too, I guess?"

"Yes. Eastwind has a few realms branching off from it, too, but nothing close to the number attached to Avalon."

He fell silent and I stared down at the table of

contents again. Were these all realm names, then? Was there a volume on these shelves that had Eastwind listed? What about one that had my home realm listed? If so, what would it be called, Earth? Did *it* have many realms branching off from it?

It was a lot to take in, but I forced myself to stay focused on the task at hand. "So I guess we need to figure out which realm this entity came from." I spoke mostly to the minotaur, who nodded. "Great, except this book is easily two thousand pages. We could be here reading for a week."

"Close. Then open," the minotaur said.

I shut my eyes, gathering my patience. "Okay, seriously. I need more help than that. You've been great so far, don't get me wrong, and this whole mysterious book cellar thing was fun and novel, but I really need—"

"Close. Then open."

I cleared my throat to collect myself. I was *not* big on men interrupting me, but when a dead one with a bull's head who stood a cool two feet taller than myself did it, I figured it was not the best time to launch into a lecture on male privilege.

I closed the book.

Then I opened it.

Pages fluttered open with the front cover, and when I looked down at the one it opened to, I almost dropped the dang thing in surprise.

A detailed hand-drawn image of the battlefield stared back at me from the old parchment pages.

"Whoa," said Donovan. "That's lucky."

The minotaur lifted his snout in a self-satisfied way as he crossed his arms.

"Yeah, yeah," I said, then turned my attention to the page, reading every word I could about the battle of the two armies, the blue rain god and the white wind god summoned by the smaller army, and then finally, I saw what I was looking for. "Ba," I breathed. Donovan's chest was pressed against my shoulder as he read along.

"That's got to be it," he said. He pointed to a passage as he read. "Commander Feingart, knowing his men would lose when blinded by the rain and facing into the wind, did the only thing he could to stand a chance, though ultimately it was what lost him the war. He summoned Ba, the unwieldy and insatiable drought god to fight off the twin deities summoned by Admiral Glom. Ba made quick work of the others, but when Feingart lost control of her, she turned on his army and stole all their water, wine, and made the earth before them inhospitable to growing food, starving the Dym army and costing them the war." He glanced up at me. "Drought? Unwieldy? Stealing water, ruining crops? I think this might be our entity."

"Unfortunately, I think you're right." The minotaur left us alone then, returning to whatever business he was attending when we'd shown up. "But that also means our entity is a god. That doesn't work in our favor."

"Not necessarily. It says god because that's what these people believed it was. But it could just as easily be another kind of powerful entity—a demon or phantom."

"Geez, I never thought I'd be relieved to know I was facing *just* a demon. So, how do we get rid of it?"

He motioned for me to hand him the book, which I did, and then he turned to the next page. "It says the Hon army was eventually able to banish the Ba by calling for

an oracle who performed the following incantation ..."
He turned the page and swore.

I immediately understood why. The incantation was long, required a grocery store's worth of ingredients, and was probably beyond Donovan's level of expertise.

"Can we get all this at the Pixie Mixie?" I asked.

"Maybe. All except one thing."

"Which is what?"

"An oracle."

"Oh." Yeah, Kayleigh probably didn't have one of those in stock. "Is there an oracle in Eastwind? Surely there is. You have one of everything I can think of and then some. For example, I'd never even heard of a were-elk before I came here. Yet, there one is, handing out citations to juveniles and eating apple pie daily."

"No, there are no oracles in Eastwind. There might be one or two in Avalon, but they require special care usually, and Eastwind doesn't have the resources."

I scanned the incantation. "Does it explicitly say that it has to be an oracle who does this spell?"

He checked again. "Huh. No, I guess not. I just assumed because they used one to trap her the first time."

"Great. No oracle required, far as I'm concerned."

He narrowed his eyes my direction, tilting his head like a confused puppy. "It's almost as if you're *trying* to get yourself killed." He rested a hand on my shoulder. "Between us, Nora, are you suicidal?"

I stepped away from him quickly. "What? No! I just don't have the time to hunt down an oracle! Besides, it's not like Ba has caused any harm to humans."

He shook his head minutely, blinking rapidly. "What's a human?"

"It's, um, like a witch but without magic. Forget it. I just mean you and I might not be at any risk. Sure, it might make us super thirsty, but—"

"You do realize we're made up almost entirely of water, right?"

I snapped my mouth shut. I did know that. And I'd considered it as a possible danger. But I was hoping Donovan wouldn't arrive at that reality yet. I grumbled, "*Now* who's constructing obstacles?"

He grunted not unlike Anton. Except Donovan's grunt had a single clear meaning. He was caving. "Fine, but remember what I said. I *will* haunt you. It won't be fun. Say goodbye to privacy."

"Creep."

He shrugged.

"Okay, so I guess we just copy down the spell on a piece of paper and take it with us since this book ain't going anywhere anytime soon?" I tugged at the chain.

"Do you have a piece of paper?" he asked.

"No, but I'm sure we can find one."

He shoved the book back at me. "No need." Reaching behind him, he pulled his wand from his waistband and touched the tip to the page. The words of the incantation glowed, and as he drew his wand away from the paper, the glowing words followed through the air behind until they floated in front of us. Then, with a flick of his wrist, they disappeared. "I can pull them back up when I need them."

"Wow. You're like a *witch* witch."

"As opposed to?"

"Me, I guess."

He nodded. "Yeah, I definitely come out on top in that comparison."

I thanked the minotaur on our way out (he didn't even look up from his book), and let Donovan lead the way through the tunnels, up into the main gallery of the library. I was glad someone had paid attention to the route we'd taken, because I sure hadn't. As much as I hated to admit it, I was, deep down, glad I had Donovan with me.

Chapter Eleven

"I'm trying not to get psyched out that most of the ingredients we need are in the necromancy section," I whispered to Donovan as we collected our supplies from the Pixie Mixie.

"You and me both," he said. "If we have to rely mostly on your magic, we're both dead."

"Uncalled for," I said, grabbing a jar of dragon blood from the shelf and inspecting it. "Doesn't seem like this should be legal."

"Don't worry," he replied, "the dragons are compensated quite well for their donations. Look at the price tag."

I turned over the jar and almost dropped it. "Sweet baby jackalope. This stuff has gotta be worth more per ounce than gold."

"It is."

"And how much of it do we need?"

"Just a few drops."

I replaced the jar on the shelf like it was a rigged

bomb and grabbed a tiny dropper next to it, which still cost almost a week's worth of tips from Medium Rare. "There's not a substitute?" I said. "Maybe a close replacement?"

"You want a close replacement for the incantation, or you want the actual incantation?"

I gritted my teeth and put the dragon's blood into Donovan's basket. I had the money, that wasn't the issue. The issue was that I'd have rather saved it for something else. Like my own house.

Kayleigh Lytefoot grinned at us and, on the whole, did an admirable job of acting like she wasn't confused about why Donovan and I were shopping in the necromancy section together. But as she jotted down the items one at a time, her facade started to crumble. "I know it's none of my business," she said, "but I just want to make sure you two know what you're getting into before you experiment with this sort of thing."

"I appreciate the concern," Donovan said. "And I assure you, we really don't have a clue what we're getting into. But Nora likes it best that way."

Kayleigh paused, her eyes jumping from Donovan to me, then a sly grin turned the corners of her lips. "Yes, Stella is the same way. I don't understand it myself, but I do know that it's not always a bad thing. Being in a relationship with it, though, can be tricky." She pressed her lips together and cast Donovan a cautionary look.

"Oh, no," I said, jumping to the side to put distance between Donovan and myself. "We're not in a relationship."

"Mm-hmm," she said, no longer paying attention as

she jotted down the final items in her ledger. "Will you be paying in full today, or should I bill you?"

I cringed. "Bill me, please. I'm good for it. I just don't carry that much gold around with me."

She nodded, grinning brightly. "You would be murdered pretty instantly if you did. I'll send the receipt by owl to Ruby's house. You still live there, right?"

"Yeah ..." I grimaced. "But if you could wait, like, a day before sending it over ...?" I hoped I didn't have to spell out the rest, the part about how if Ruby saw the inventory on the receipt before I could complete the incantation, she would probably lose her mind and drag me out of the Deadwoods before I could accomplish what I'd just spent a fortune to do.

"Are you *sure* you need to do this?" Kayleigh asked as she held out handles of the canvas bag of supplies.

I grabbed it from her and lugged it off the counter. "Mostly. Thanks, Kayleigh. Tell Stella I said hello. I still owe her one for the help a couple weeks ago." Stella Lytefoot, Kayleigh's life partner, was Eastwind's top potions master and had done a solid for Tanner, Grim, and me when a taste enhancement potion had gone horribly awry.

"Don't worry about that," Kayleigh replied as Donovan and I reached the front door. "Just try not to get yourself killed, okay?"

Dusk was settling on Eastwind when Grim trotted up from where he'd parked it in some soft, cool grass outside the apothecary.

"I take it Kayleigh doesn't know about you and Tanner," said Donovan.

"No. Why would I tell *her*?" I snapped.

Whoa, Nora, rein it in.

"Sorry," I said. "It's just, well, you know."

"I really don't." He grabbed the straps of the canvas bag, pulling it off my shoulder and hoisting it up onto his.

As we passed a few familiar faces along our route, I wondered how long it would take before Tanner heard about Donovan and I enjoying an evening of shopping on the town.

"It's just a typical petty woman thing," I said. "I'm sure it doesn't surprise you that I would have a typical petty woman thing."

"Actually," he said, "it does. You don't strike me as petty. Or typical."

"Then let me ask you something. Who do you think Kayleigh looks like?"

Donovan's face pinched in toward his nose as he stared out over the buildings down the hill of us in the direction of the Outskirts. "Never thought about it."

"She looks like me," I said quickly.

He paused, turning to squint down at me. His detailed inspection of me from head to foot made me itch to escape his view. But I made sure not to show it. "Ah, yeah, I could see that," he concluded.

"Right." I looked away from him before a blush overtook my face and started back down the street. "Not only that, but despite being hundreds of years older than me, she's the prettier, younger version of me."

"I don't know about that," he said.

"No, it's fine. Every woman discovers one eventually —a younger, prettier, maybe even more talented version of herself who's probably super nice and impossible to hate, which only makes us hate her more. I knew this day would come, I just didn't expect her to be an ancient pixie."

"You're being incredibly stupid," he said, in usual form. But then he added, "You're way hotter than she is."

I nearly gagged on my own spit. I wanted to say something, but I didn't know what.

Maybe you should say nothing for once.

Now there was a novel idea.

"Oh great," he said, "are you going to be all awkward about that now?"

"I'm not being awkward about anything."

"You absolutely are. I admitted that I thought you were hot, and then, for the first time since I've known you, you don't hurl an insult my way. Ergo, you're being awkward."

"What am I supposed to say, 'Thanks, Donovan, I think you're hot, too'?"

He chuckled. "Wouldn't hurt. I like compliments as much as the next witch."

"Please, like you don't have women throwing themselves at you. Mr. Sexy Bartender with a tortured soul and emotional walls so high a weregazelle on a trampoline couldn't clear them. I know your type."

"Oh yeah? You think I'm a type?" he said bitterly.

"Totally. *And* you would've been just my type before I came to Eastwind."

"But not anymore."

"Nope. Not anymore. Because New Nora is not a self-sabotaging masochist like Old Nora was."

He shook his head, sighing. "Wow. You think someone would have to be a self-sabotaging masochist to want to be with me? For fang's sake, remind me never to pay you another compliment."

"I didn't realize you had more than one compliment reserved for me."

"If I did before, I don't now." He adjusted the bag on his shoulder, and our conversation came to an abrupt end.

Grim spoke up from just behind me. *"Are you two going to make out or what?"*

"Ew, Grim. No."

"I'm just asking, because if you are, I could use a bathroom break."

"Hold it until the Deadwoods. We're almost there."

"I make no promises."

"We should take the long way around," I said once Medium Rare came into view. "When Tanner heard you and I were spending the night together"—I shook my head—"the evening. Spending the evening together. Whatever. He decided to work late."

Donovan nodded, and we took a detour to avoid being seen.

The plan was to follow the drought path, which wasn't hard to make out, even from twenty yards off. While the Deadwoods contained plenty of dead things, the plants themselves were very much alive, except for where Ba had passed. We would simply follow the dried and wilted path, and with any luck, it would take us past Ted's house. It hadn't been difficult to conclude his was the house we'd seen in the vision. Not only because the grim reaper was one of the few people able to live in the Deadwoods without worrying about the innumerable threats, but also because the odds of there being more than one Deadwood inhabitant who spent his or her free time building birdhouses seemed slim to none.

His home would serve as a checkpoint to show we were on the right path, but ultimately, we would have to proceed farther, deeper into the secluded forest until we reached the misty tunnel of trees. And then what? I had a hunch, but I planned on feeling it out once, or rather *if*, we got there.

Entering the Deadwoods was like pressing mute on everything Eastwind. I wasn't two steps past the tree line when all of the ambient noise of Eastwind I'd long since stopped noticing—the birds, the chatter, the occasional clamor of cartwheels over cobblestone—disappeared entirely. I glanced over my shoulder and spied the light of Medium Rare, shining through the late dusk, and was that Tanner's figure in the window? But I couldn't hear any of the familiar sounds.

I remembered when I'd stood in this exact spot and seen Eastwind for the first time. Though back then, I'd assumed I was still in Texas. The smell of the diner food had drawn me in and taken me back to memories of the diner I used to visit with my parents as a child. A lifetime ago.

"You okay, Nora?"

I turned my back on Eastwind. Donovan was staring at me expectantly. "Huh? Yeah, I'm fine."

"You'll see it again," he said.

"I know." I walked farther into the woods, shoulder-to-shoulder with him.

"You looked like you *didn't* know."

"No, it wasn't that. I was just thinking."

"About?"

Normally, I'd have told him to mind his own business, but the strangeness of having memories from two different lives was clouding my judgment. "Just the first time I saw Eastwind. I was standing right there."

"Wait, but that means you entered Eastwind through—"

"The Deadwoods. You didn't know that? Yep. I saw Medium Rare and wandered to it. It was almost like I was led there. And I guess I was, since I'd followed in the direction Grim disappeared after he'd woken me up."

"And then you met Tanner," he finished. "I guess I can see why you have a thing for him. First point of contact, and all."

"You make it sound like some sort of psychological syndrome."

"Love usually is."

"It's not love," I said.

He chuckled. "Okay." Then he picked up the pace and I hurried to keep up.

"You don't believe me?"

"I'm just saying, I've seen the way women fall for Tanner, and it's always fast and hard."

"How many women ... No, never mind. I don't want to know."

"You're the first he's been interested in, for what it's worth, which is part of the reason I don't understand why you two are hiding it from everyone."

"To be fair, it's mostly me that's hiding it. Tanner doesn't care if people know."

He chuckled. "I figured. So, why don't you want people to know?"

"It complicates things."

"And takes you off the market."

I jerked my head around to glare at him. "That doesn't matter to me."

"You said yourself, you were a self-sabotaging masochist in your past life. Maybe some of Old Nora stuck around, and *she* is interested in other people."

"Not a chance," I said. "You're just projecting your own issues onto me."

He shrugged. "Very likely. I have enough to go around."

"And why *is* that? I hear your family is highly respected. As we accidentally established, you're hot. Why don't *you* have a girlfriend? Or do you? Ooh, maybe a secret one? Maybe *that's* why it bothers you that Tanner has one, too."

"You're so right," he said dramatically. "What have I been thinking all this time? I'm not an orphan, so I shouldn't have any issues."

"I didn't say that."

"You basically did. But that's fine. You want to know what my problem is? Tanner. Tanner is my problem. He's my best friend, and he's the biggest problem in my life."

I didn't understand, but then I remembered how nicely decorated Donovan's home was. Ugh. Grim was probably right. "You're in love with him," I said.

Donovan froze then slowly turned his entire body to face me. "No. I'm not in love with him. Wait, you think I'm gay?"

I winced. "Maybe?"

He rolled his eyes. "No, Nora. I'm not gay and I'm not in love with Tanner. It's more complicated than that. I shouldn't have said anything about it."

"No," I said, jogging to catch him as he set forward again. "Explain, please. I'm sorry I made assumptions."

"You wouldn't understand anyway."

"Try me."

He adjusted the heavy canvas bag on his shoulder and sighed. "I'm single because I can't get anyone to stick around."

I bit my tongue to stay silent and let him continue.

"Tanner's always been there for me, and we've been friends since we were little. I even knew his parents before they were killed. He's the best guy I know. And that's the problem. Growing up, I could always snag the girl I wanted, but eventually she would get to know Tanner and fall head over heels for him. I couldn't compete. He was either oblivious to the girl's feelings for him or knew but showed no interest. Because he's so nice, it always took the girls a while to catch on. Sometimes they would come crawling back to me, but mostly they would move on.

"I'm just not made like him. I can't connect with people that easily. I don't know how to express my emotions like he does. I can't make friends the way he can. I'm not going to stop being friends with him because he's a better person than I am, but I get a little tired of him always being the standard I'm compared to.

"So, of course, if he's your first contact in Eastwind, and then you meet me, yeah, you're going to hate me. I expected that from the start."

"I don't hate you."

"Right."

"What? I don't. Even though you've been a complete jerk to me since I first set foot in Franco's Pizza. You're just projecting again. If anyone here hates anyone else, it's you hating me."

He tilted his head back, shutting his eyes tight. "Are you *kidding* me?" He turned to me. "I don't hate you, Nora. How do you not understand? You have the same walls, too." He rested a hand on my shoulder. "I can feel it. You're just like me."

"The hell I am," I said sharply, shrugging his hand off of me and hurrying after Grim who was, smartly, remaining far enough ahead to ignore the conversation taking place behind him.

"Nora!" he called after me.

"Hush!" came Grim's voice in my head.

"Hush!" I said, relaying the message to Donovan.

My familiar had paused, one paw pointing as he scented the air.

"What is it?" I asked.

"Get behind me. Close," he insisted.

I turned to Donovan and waved him over impatiently as I hurried to catch up to Grim. The two of us waited, and I strained through the silence, listening for what had raised Grim's hackles.

"Something there?" Donovan whispered.

I shot him a fierce glare, putting my finger to my lips before mouthing *wand*. I nodded down at his waistband, and he quickly complied, holding it out at arm's length as he turned in a slow circle, scanning the woods behind us. It was good thinking. Hidebehinds tended to sneak up from the rear, and it wouldn't surprise me if that were the preferred method of attack for *most* of the innumerable predators in these woods.

"It's coming this way," Grim said. *"I can smell it."*

"What is it?"

"Not sure yet. We'll know soon enough."

A moment that felt like a lifetime later, something massive rustled in the bushes ahead and to the left. Grim growled low, and Donovan put his wand at the ready. I'd never felt so useless in my life. No wand, no fangs, only a few half-hearted self-defense classes when I first moved to downtown Austin. A lot of good *that* would do against whatever unmentionable thing was stalking us now.

Then it burst from the shadows in a quick, clumsy leap and paused only a handful of yards off, staring at us with dumb recognition.

"It's just an elk," Donovan said, starting to lower his wand.

I reached forward and pushed his hand back up again. "Don't be fooled. I had a friend who was almost killed by an elk. They're dumb and dangerous." Although, admittedly, I was relieved it was an animal I recognized instead of one I didn't have a name for. But then I started to doubt myself. "Wait, that *is* just a regular elk, right? It's not going to shoot fireballs out of its antlers or anything?"

Donovan stared down at me like I was crazy. "That's not a thing."

"It's not a regular elk," said Grim. *"It's a were-elk. And if the lingering smell of coffee and pie on its breath is any indication ..."*

"Deputy Manchester?" I said, taking a step forward.

"No kidding?" said Donovan, lowering his wand again.

The elk exhaled in a huff and nodded politely. Then a second later, he galloped off into the darkness.

"After the day he had, I don't blame him for wanting to blow off a little steam," Donovan said. "Since Eastwind is so uptight about shifted forms, werewolves and shifters have to come out here to let loose. I've heard Friday nights are quite the free-for-all out here."

"Every night is a free-for-all out here, pretty boy," Grim groused.

"We'll probably owe him an explanation for why we're out here," Donovan said, "but if running into Stu Manchester is the worst that happens out here, we should consider ourselves lu—"

He disappeared in a flash, and were it not for the snarling and his yell, I would have thought he'd vanished into thin air.

The dark thing obscured Donovan's body almost entirely from view. Was that Ba? Had it been waiting for us?

But Ba had maintained a smoke-like form in the vision, the one I was accustomed to seeing in spirits. Whatever was on top of Donovan, who kicked and fought from his position on the ground, was solid as the trees around us.

Grim attacked, fangs bared, and were I not so confused and terrified, I might have been impressed. For all the talk Grim had done about being a dangerous beast, I'd only once before seen any hint of it.

He crashed into the beast from the side, sending it tumbling across the crunchy forest floor. Donovan scrambled to his feet, searching around for something on the ground. "My wand! Where is my—"

Another figure tackled him from the other side, and

his yelp was muffled by a ton of black fur I could only just make out.

Grim? But, no, Grim was still tussling with the original beast that had tackled Donovan.

"Hellhounds!" Grim shouted. *"There'll be a third on the way, Nora! Keep a look out!"*

"And do what?" If the third showed up, I didn't exactly have a way to defend myself.

A howl rose up behind me, turning my blood to ice. The other two hellhounds froze, climbing off of Grim and Donovan to stand tall and reply with their own howl.

"Oh poop," Grim said.

"What? What is it?!"

"I know these jerks. Hold on, give me a second."

As he strode toward the new arrival—the largest of the pack by about a foot in every direction—I hurried over to help Donovan back to his feet. "You okay?" I whispered, grabbing him under his armpits to get him up.

He stared wide-eyed at Grim and the hellhounds, saying nothing as the canines barked and growled back and forth. So I checked him for any injuries and found only a few raised claw marks down his arms. We'd need to wash those off for sure, but the beast hadn't drawn blood. As I wiped the leaves and twigs off his back, he whispered, "What's happening?"

"I think Grim knows them," I said.

"Is that good?"

"I have no idea. They stopped attacking, didn't they?"

"True. I can't complain."

When Grim trotted over to us again (the fact that he was willing to turn his back to them seemed a good sign), he said, *"Looks like it's our lucky day."*

"Meaning?"

"First of all, Donovan bore the brunt of the attack rather than you or me. Also, they've offered to guard us the rest of the way."

"What? How did you manage that?"

"What's he saying?" Donovan demanded. I waved at him to shut up for a second.

"*Ba has been making their life difficult,*" Grim explained. "*Acher Lake is the main water source in their pack's territory, and that thirsty demon drank it up. I told them we were going to stop it and if we did, the water would come back.*"

"We don't know the water will come back."

"*Sure, but they don't know that we don't know that. They're just a bunch of dumb hounds. Only speak in barks and growls. Very limiting language means very limited understanding of how things work. To be honest, I almost forgot how to speak it.*"

"What happens if we defeat the entity and the water doesn't come back?"

Grim snapped at a fly that buzzed around his snout, his eye crossing and teeth clacking as he missed. "*Then we lie and tell them it takes a day. And we hustle out of the Deadwoods and don't come back until they forget all about it.*"

"You said you knew them. Did they used to be your pack?" He certainly looked almost identical, though he would be the runt of the litter.

"*Pfft. No way. Yes, I was technically a hellhound before I became a grim, but I never would've run with those idiots. Hellhounds travel in packs of three, so they're all set anyway.*"

"What happened to your pack when you died? Did they get a third member?"

Grim reared up, tilting his head back to stare down at me. "You sure right now, in the middle of the Deadwoods, is the best moment to suddenly take an interest in my life?"

"Good point. But on the other hand, we might die soon, so this could be my only chance."

"That's what I like about you, Nora. You're an optimist."

I filled Donovan in on the new development as we approached the three hellhounds ahead of us in the drought path. If his fist gripping his wand was any indication, he was not entirely sure he trusted the hounds to keep their word.

Grim took the lead, and when I glanced over my shoulder, the two smaller hounds went off in either direction to flank us, disappearing into the darkness. The giant alpha remained behind, planted where it was as we continued forward. I turned my attention ahead to keep from running into something, and the next time I looked behind me, the alpha was nowhere to be seen.

Chapter Twelve

❧❧❧

"Quiet now, unless you want to spend the rest of the night playing bridge and having night veil tea pushed on you," said Grim as we approached the shack where Ted lived. It looked exactly the same as in the vision with the birdhouses (which I happened to know were fireproof) hanging from the trees surrounding it. I did not, in fact, want to play bridge with Death, so I did as Grim suggested and tiptoed past Ted's house, giving it a wide berth.

I'd once read that humans used to be nocturnal, as evidenced by the rods in our eyes that help us see at night. I didn't know if the same held for witches—or really where I stood on the evolutionary map, to be honest—but it sure felt like I was accessing some long-dormant ability as I managed to avoid falling flat on my face, despite how little moonlight made it in through the thick treetops.

The Deadwoods also held a darkness to them that wasn't precisely visual. No, I'm not talking metaphorically here. I'm still being literal. But it wasn't like normal darkness. It was just a cloud of black that seemed present in every square inch of the space, smothering the possibility of more light.

The trail of drought-withered plants sloped downward sharply into a ditch, and I paused to assess the feasibility of walking into it.

"They weren't kidding," Grim muttered, standing beside me.

"Who wasn't kidding?"

"The hellhounds. This ditch used to be Acher Lake. But it looks like someone got thirsty." He strolled down the steep bank without trouble, flaunting the versatility of having four legs.

"Are we getting close?" Donovan asked once we were down into the empty ditch.

"He's awfully impatient to get himself killed," said Grim.

"I think we're getting close," I replied, ignoring my familiar.

Speaking of getting oneself killed, that was exactly what was waiting for me if I didn't get my head on straight. I should've been concentrating on the complex incantation ahead, clearing my mind, honing my focus, maybe keeping some semblance of situational awareness so I didn't get dragged off by a hidebehind or shifted werewolf. Sure, the hellhounds said they would prowl the perimeter around us, but I didn't know how capable they were or even that we could trust them to stick to their word.

Instead, I kept thinking about the conversation with

Donovan, the one I'd put an abrupt end to when it started to get too real.

Oh boy, I was a cliche. *I'm not closed off! You're closed off! End of story!* I certainly wouldn't be winning an award for introspection anytime soon. Not like that, at least. As much as I'd wanted the old me to die when I did, I knew deep down that it didn't work that way. I woke up in Eastwind with the same memories, same fears, and same issues as I'd always had. I couldn't quit me cold turkey. And maybe I couldn't quit me at all.

What if I *wanted* to be the kind of girl who Tanner would fall for, but I just wasn't? Donovan's struggles resonated, as little as I liked to admit it. I had never been warm. I'd earned people's respect, but rarely their admiration or friendship. No one had ever rooted for me like everyone did Tanner. Generosity and consideration of others wasn't a natural instinct. I'd learned it, sure, and was glad I had, but it took more effort than I thought it should.

Maybe I'd always gone for guys like Donovan because they were like me, because they would understand all those things and not expect more from me than I could give, not push me to be something other than what came naturally. And maybe that was okay. It was entirely possible I hadn't found the right guy not because I went for the wrong type, but because of any number of other factors—they worked different hours, they lived too far away, they were already in love with someone else. Anything.

"Hey," I said, breaking the silence. "You sure you're okay?"

He nodded.

"You got tackled pretty good back there."

"Twice."

"I was worried about you, I thought you might—"

His head whipped around and he shot me an ice-cold glare that made the words fall dead in my throat. Okay, maybe I deserved that. But I also needed him to listen. We couldn't keep moving forward on our mission if we weren't on good terms.

And maybe I felt guilty.

So I pressed on. "I want to apologize for what I said back there. I didn't mean to make you feel like ... I don't know."

He kept his eyes ahead of us now, purposefully avoiding my gaze. "Like there was something wrong with me?"

"Yeesh, is that what I did?"

"Pretty much."

"If it makes you feel any better, I did sort of prove your point about how I haven't changed."

He laughed in a heavy exhale before reining it in. "I hadn't thought about it like that."

"I'm surprised. You're usually so quick to pinpoint my faults."

He shot me a side glance and nudged me with his elbow. "You mean like how you're all up in the Deadwoods wanting to talk about your feelings rather than focusing on the task at hand?"

"Ahh, there it is. Phew, I was worried you were losing your touch." I met his eyes and grinned.

He chuckled, shaking his head. "You're something else, Nora Ashcroft."

"We're here," said Grim.

I held out my arm to stop Donovan. "There it is."

The dark tunnel of trees stood ahead of us, beckoning us to enter. But what lay beyond was a mystery not even our magical visions had divulged.

"And you say you don't know what's on the other side?" I asked Grim again.

"Nope. There's an entire forest for me to explore, so why would I choose to enter through the terrifying and obviously cursed tunnel of doom?"

"No need to be so ominous."

"Did you just tell a walking death omen to stop being ominous? That's like asking you to stop pushing people away."

"Don't you start with me."

"True. We should get on good terms quick since we're both about to die. There's a good chance I'll come back as King of the Grims or something, but you'll probably just be dead dead."

"What's he saying?" Donovan asked. "I can tell you two are communicating. You get this little wrinkle in your forehead." He pointed at it, and I swatted his hand away.

"We were talking about how we're all going to die."

One of his eyebrows hitched up slightly. "So you *can* die? Because I was wondering about that. I mean, you died once, and then you came here. Grim's already died, so I figured he might not have to worry about death either. Which just left me."

"Hold up. You came out here even though you sort of suspected you were the only one in legit mortal danger?"

He stared down at the ground as if embarrassed by his own bravery. "Yeah, so?"

That didn't seem very Donovan of Donovan. Maybe

there was more to him than I'd given him credit for. "So that's the stupidest thing I've ever heard."

His head jerked up and he glared at me, but before he could spat something mean, I cut him off with, "Don't worry, I love stupid things."

"*You're simply delaying the inevitable,*" hollered Grim from the tunnel entrance. "*Can we get on with it?*"

Donovan moved closer, moving his hand toward my face, grinning mischievously. He dragged his pointed finger down the center of my forehead. "There it is. The crease. What'd he say now?"

I swallowed hard. My heart raced, and not just because of the imminent threat of mortal danger. Donovan's blue eyes cut through the gloom like a knife. "He says we're just delaying the inevitable and can we get on with it?"

Traces of the energy we'd shared during our connection ritual passed from his soft, warm fingertips to my jawline as he brushed a piece of hair out of my face, tucking it behind my ear. "And which inevitable thing is he talking about?"

My mouth went dry like I'd eaten a handful of chalk. "Death," I croaked, then I inhaled and took a quick step back. "I'm fairly sure he's talking about death. Probably a painful one, too."

"Right." Donovan cleared his throat, letting his hand fall back to his side. "Then let's get to it."

Chapter Thirteen

"I'll go first," I said, but Donovan grabbed my arm before I could enter the tunnel.

"Don't be an idiot. You don't even have a wand." He pushed ahead, his wand held out in front of him, and within a few steps, the darkness of the tunnel swallowed him up.

I hurried forward, not wanting to leave him on his own whenever he made it out the other side. *If* he made it out the other side.

But before I did, I glanced back to make sure Grim wasn't going to pull a quick one and desert us. His feet remained planted in place. *"Oh, please don't tell me the future King of the Grims is scared to enter."*

"I won't because that's not the case. I'm just mulling over my options."

"How hard can that be? You either come with us or you abandon us."

"Hush, woman. It's more complicated than that. I wouldn't expect you to understand."

"Understand what?"

He grunted, staring intensely at one of the bent trees. Then, after muttering, *"Aw screw it. Let's do this,"* he hiked his hind leg and began unloading on the tunnel entrance.

"Really? You have to do that right now?"

"See? I knew you wouldn't understand. Marking this doom tunnel is probably the highlight of my marking career, and here you are turning up your nose at it."

"Please don't talk to me while you're doing that," I said. *"Just promise you'll follow whenever you've emptied the tank."*

"Promise. If I die for real, I'll be going out on a high note now. And, hopefully, marking my territory on an extremely powerful and possibly sacred location isn't what tips the scales against us."

I'd always suspected Grim would be the death of me. Maybe that was just my innate bias against death omens, but I thought it was something more specific than that.

I pushed ahead, hurrying to catch up with Donovan despite not being able to see past my fingertips as I held them out in front of me, feeling the way.

What if Donovan made it to the end and something was waiting for us, and by the time I made it, he was already dead, torn limb from limb or—

No point in worrying if I could do something to prevent it. I picked up my pace, moving at an awkward high-stepping jog to make sure I didn't trip on any of the dead branches I knew to be there only by feel as I came upon them. I tried not to think about what else might be in the space below my knees, crawling or slithering around silently.

My arms hit something solid and my reaction time was too slow. I plowed right into it, and it hissed, "Ram's horn, Nora!"

"Oh, sorry."

He pressed against me, resting a hand on my waist to anchor himself, and I could feel his warm breath on my face, though I couldn't see him in the pitch blackness. "Why are you running? Are you okay?"

"Yeah, I'm fine. I just wanted to catch up so you didn't have to face whatever is up ahead on your own."

He said nothing and his hand slipped from my waist down to my hand, taking it in his. I gripped it tight so I didn't lose him again, and we crept forward. "Can't you make that thing light up?" I said.

"Sure. I can also make it wail like a siren, if you're super into announcing our presence to anything nearby."

I refrained from replying, because he did make a solid point.

Time was a tricky thing to hold onto with my sense of sight deprived, and I couldn't tell how many minutes passed before a dim light appeared ahead.

We paused at the end of the tunnel to take in the new surroundings. I didn't quite know what to make of them.

Ahead of us was a rocky clearing surrounded on three sides by gigantic trees, and on the side farthest from us, ocean spread out to the horizon, reflecting the light of a full moon. The sound of crashing waves slowly faded into my consciousness. "I didn't know Eastwind was a coastal town," I whispered.

"It's not," replied Donovan.

"Then where are we?"

His hand squeezed mine tighter. I'd forgotten I was

still holding onto him, but considering the strange and uncertain circumstances we now found ourselves, I wasn't keen on letting go.

"I think we just entered another realm," he breathed.

"Have you ever entered another realm?"

"Just Avalon. I was a kid, though."

"Should we turn back?" I asked.

"Not yet." He stuck out his chest, let go of my hand, and entered into this new realm we knew nothing about.

It was like he wanted to die.

And maybe I did, too, because I followed right behind him.

Our progress was slow as we crept toward the edge of the clearing overlooking the ocean. A stone circle lay up ahead, not far from the edge, and I knew that was the place to go. Maybe Donovan knew it too, because he made straight for it.

At the center was a small fire pit, and once we were near enough, I noticed the glowing embers.

So did Donovan. He whirled around, putting his back to the circle and cliff, scanning the clearing we'd just crossed before inspecting the edge of the dense forest.

These trees were nothing like the Deadwoods. They were evergreens, towering easily twice the height of the ones we'd just trekked through.

And between them, I saw nothing.

Then I heard the recognizable crunch of footsteps.

Donovan eased the canvas bag off his shoulder and onto one of the stones before shutting his eyes and muttered something. Then with a flick of his wrist, a ball of light shot out of his wand, zipping for the trees, where it weaved and circled around trunks until I heard a yelp, and out popped two figures. The light from Donovan's wand hovered over them, illuminating their guilty faces.

"Are you kidding me?" he said, stomping toward them. "Can you two get any dumber?"

Tybalt's shoulders hunched in an appropriate display of shame, but Duncan remained defiant, wearing that same unapologetic snarl that I'd seen back in Medium Rare after he'd just grabbed my butt.

"What are you doing here?" Duncan said.

"Cleaning up after your mess, obviously. What do *you* think you're doing?"

"Th-the same," Tybalt stammered. "We didn't mean for it to get so out of hand. We only meant—"

Donovan smacked him on the side of the head, cutting his lame excuse short. "That's for conjuring a drought god."

"Ow!" Tybalt clutched his head.

Donovan smacked the smugness off Duncan's face with a swift bop up-side his dome. "And that's for harassing Nora."

"Hey," I said, approaching, "I wanted to do that."

"Sorry, Mr. Stringfellow," said Tybalt remorsefully. "I didn't realize she was your girl."

"Um, she's not. But she doesn't have to be my girl, or anyone's girl, for it to be totally inappropriate for you to go into her place of work and sexually harass and assault her."

"Yeah," I said, lunging forward to get a quick smack in on the other side of Tybalt's head.

"But physical assault is okay?" he whined, holding a hand on each side of his head now.

"No, I guess not," I replied.

But Donovan jumped in with, "Of course it's okay, if you're being a numbskull and a little painful reminder keeps you from getting yourself killed. Do you have any idea what the thing you conjured has done to Eastwind?" His voice shook with rage. I'd never seen him like that. The bitter sarcasm and calm-but-biting jabs were obliterated by his raw anger.

"Of course we know. Why else would we be out here, genius?" said Duncan.

Donovan raised his wand. "If you really knew what you were up against, you wouldn't have come out here yourself. You would have turned yourself in to the Coven and let them handle it. Instead, you cocky little twerps think you can come out here and take it on. You don't even have your wands yet!" His lip curled into a snarl.

Tybalt trembled, but Duncan remained standoffish. "*She* doesn't have a wand," he said, pointing to me. "You came out here and your only backup is a female witch who's never been to Mancer and doesn't own a wand. Maybe you're just as stupid as us."

"Nora could kick your foolish hide any day of the week, wand or no wand. And I can guarantee you she's already a better witch than either of you two dunces will ever be. What were you thinking, conjuring a drought god?"

"We didn't mean to!" Tybalt protested. "We meant to conjure a simple wight, resurrect something harmless from beyond to just give her a scare." Donovan's nostrils flared and he shuffled a half-step toward Tybalt. "It was his idea!" the blond kid spat, ratting out his friend.

"Who cares whose idea it was?" Donovan growled. "You went along with it. Necromancy! You two honestly thought you might turn out to be Fifth Wind witches? That you might have control over the dead?"

"It could happen," said Duncan, crossing his arms. "If she can do it without any training, why can't we?"

"The answer is so obvious, I'm gonna let you two figure it out." Donovan eased up, backing off and inhaling deeply as he tucked his wand into his waistband. "Also, by the way, congratulations, you're clearly East Wind witches." He shook his head. "I'm embarrassed to share that distinction with you two, but there you have it."

"Huh?" Tybalt scrunched up his face. "How do you know we're East Wind witches? We haven't gotten to that level yet."

"Your pathetic attempt at necromancy brought over a demon that kills by sucking water from things. It's not a difficult logical leap. Now how about the two of you get the fang out of here and try not to get yourself killed on the way back through the Deadwoods? And then each of you go to your respective homes and hope that Nora and I don't get *ourselves* killed fixing this mess, because I can guarantee we will make a point to haunt you if we do."

I tried not to laugh at Donovan overextending himself with all the hauntings he was promising. Also, I decided not to point out that haunting a couple teenaged boys, catching glimpses of them when they thought they were alone in the privacy of their bedrooms, was one hundred percent my idea of hell.

"Go. Now," Donovan said, reaching back for his wand again.

Tybalt took charge, shoving Duncan toward the entrance to the tunnel leading to Eastwind. Once he was in motion, Duncan had no problem running at a full-out sprint. He was noticeably faster than Tybalt and had no problem leaving his friend in his dust without looking back.

Just before the boys reached tunnel, a dark figure emerged. A dark, fluffy figure.

Duncan slid to a stop and screamed.

"What the what?!" shouted Grim as he was confronted by a screaming manboy charging straight at him. His tail flew between his legs as he jumped to the side.

Despite the gravity of the situation, Donovan and I erupted into laughter.

"It's just her familiar," said Tybalt, whose slow pace had afforded him the luxury of distance and spared him the same jolt of shock as his buddy. "Stop being such a pixie and keep going!"

Once the boys were out of sight, Grim trotted to meet us, casting a single glance over his shoulder. *"Who were they?"*

"The ones that conjured the Ba."

"You mean the same ones who grabbed your tush?"

"Same."

"Well, shoot. If I'd know we might've run into them, I would've left more in the tank for them."

"I appreciate the sentiment, as weird as it is."

"So, now what?"

"All we have to do is perform an incantation that we're neither equipped nor knowledgeable enough to perform with any accuracy."

"Fantastic. Have fun, you two. I'll be over here making sure nothing creeps up on you while you're in that

la-la land you two rascals have been sneaking off to lately."

He found a comfortable spot on a wind-smoothed boulder between the stone circle and the rest of the clearing, and flopped down.

The odds of him remaining awake seemed slim.

"You ready?" I said, turning to Donovan.

He grinned at me, no hint of his usual caution. "Absolutely."

I stoked the fire with a pile of nearby wood, likely left there by Duncan and Tybalt for a later attempt at banishment, while Donovan laid out the ingredients on the canvas bag, keeping the herbs temporarily in their boxes to avoid blowing away on the ocean breeze.

Once I was finished, I had a moment to take in my surroundings and wondered what season it was here. Did this place even have seasons? It was easily ten degrees cooler than the Deadwoods had been, and the breeze sent a shiver through me as it blew against my back, sucked out to sea.

Donovan sat just to my side with the bag between us. "I think we're ready," he said, pulling out his wand, giving it a flick so that the words from the book appeared shimmering in the air. They read backward to me, but that was fine, since he would be leading this time. My job was to follow, to read his energy and move with it, offering mine up for him to use as he needed. In other words, I had to surrender myself to the incantation.

Yeah, that doesn't sound like something I'd be good at. I know.

Donovan began adding the ingredients to the flames, one by one sprinkling in each until the crackle of it had faded, then he'd add the next, reading off a series of words in that same dark language I'd heard Ruby speak in her house when Ba first entered.

When Donovan stood, so did I. He moved so that we stood opposite of each other, the small fire between us. The warmth of it was a welcome contrast to the salty wind cutting to my bones.

He drew his own blood first this time, dragging the tip of the wand across the meat of his palm. Blood splashed out, and he aimed it at the fire.

"That's a lot of blood," I said.

He nodded, flexing his fingers to draw more. Then, to my surprise, he didn't close the wound but created an identical one on the other hand, sucking in air as he let the blood drain from his other palm into the fire.

He struggled to hold his slick wand as he pointed it toward me. I offered him my hands and closed my eyes, trying not to think too much about the pain and blood loss. It would only be temporary.

But ooh boy, did it smart. I breathed through it and opened my eyes to make sure it dripped into the fire. He tucked his wand away again and held out his hands. This was it.

Then I remembered, and reached for the amulet. There was no way to avoid getting blood on my shirt as I pulled it out.

"No," said Donovan sharply. "Leave it on. I don't think you want to open yourself up that much."

"But what if it doesn't work?"

"We'll deal with that if we get to it. Please, just keep that thing on you, okay?"

I nodded, letting it drop down to rest on the

bloodstained fabric of my shirt, then I reached out for him. Our clasped bloody hands reflected the firelight, glowing like two hot coals as he nodded to me gently and we closed our eyes.

He must have committed the incantation to memory as he recited it without the help of his notes. He droned on and on before I realized he was repeating the same few phrases over and over again. I focused my attention on the sounds, and slowly I was able to repeat the phrases along with him. At first I did it only in my mind, but once I was confident I had them down, I spoke them aloud.

And that changed everything.

The fire flared, and though I kept my eyes closed, I was sure the tips of the flames were licking our hands. The wet blood simmered on my skin, and though I knew it hurt, I didn't quite feel it.

The wind picked up, but no longer did it blow against my back. Instead, it originated between us, pushing us outward, trying to separate us as we continued our chant. But I held on tight, and so did Donovan. The foreboding of what was coming was lightened by the relief that this seemed to be working. When he raised his voice to a shout, so did I.

The waves crashing against the rocks below rose to a deafening roar, drowning out our voices, even as I yelled at the top of my lungs. I wanted to open my eyes. I needed to see Donovan's face, make sure he was still there.

Don't be silly. Of course he's still there.

I don't know why I worried, but suddenly he was squeezing my hands so tightly I felt my bones grind against each other and I suspected he'd had the same impulse.

A force rose from the flames. It strained against the small circle of our arms as it clawed its way free. My mind told me to let go of Donovan, to stop this madness, but my gut, my Insight, told me it was too late, that I had to see this thing through.

The three of us were no longer alone. The same presence I'd felt in Ruby's parlor was with us now. The chanting died in my throat and I didn't think twice before opening my eyes. A moment after I did, so did Donovan. We stared into each other's face, two people waking from a shared dream. An understanding passed between us that I couldn't put words to.

Then his gaze jumped to the side, staring past my shoulder, and he shouted, "Grim!"

Dropping one of my hands, Donovan broke the circle to grab his wand. I ducked and turned as Donovan aimed it right at me, though I wasn't worried about him harming me.

Grim was no longer resting atop the rock but rather floated over it. And above him, Ba in her terrifying dark form. This close, I could finally see her waving strands of tentacle-like hair, the dark robes that flowed around her, disappearing into a sooty, amorphous fog below her waist. It wasn't her shape that terrified me; it was the fact that the same mist we'd seen rising up from the plants in our visions was now rising from my familiar, being sucked into the black abyss of Ba.

A ball of silver light shot toward her but passed straight through. She didn't even notice it.

Donovan charged forward, sending another blast, this

time orange, at the drought god.

This one hit and sent her barrel rolling to the side just enough for Grim to drop like a sack of wet blankets to the boulder. *"I'm so thirsty …"* he moaned.

"Not now. Get out of the way before she comes back!"

He slid off the rock and stumbled to stand behind me. *"You don't have to tell me twice."*

I knew this was no good, though. Our circle had been broken. I didn't know much about the incantation, but Donovan *had* informed me that it was our connection that would muster the strength to banish the entity from Eastwind for good. But now he was facing off with Ba all by himself.

She hovered in midair, staring him down, and I held my breath. Then she turned and darted toward the tunnel.

"Stop her!" I shouted, though admittedly, I didn't have any helpful advice regarding the "how" of it.

He shot another orange ball of light at her. Then another and another. Unfortunately, his attempt to get her attention worked, and before she made it to the tunnel, she whipped around, heading straight for the dark-haired East Wind witch making an annoyance out of himself.

He struggled against her pull, but when his feet lifted off the ground and the first bit of vapor rose from his open mouth, I knew I was out of time. I didn't have a wand, but that didn't mean I was out of options.

I grabbed the amulet and slid the chain over my head, turning and slipping it onto Grim before he could resist.

Then I closed my eyes and called out to her, offering up my corporeal form.

Chapter Fourteen

My invitation to Ba was eagerly received, and I was no longer on the edge of the cliff overlooking a strange ocean.

The crashing waves had disappeared, replaced by birds chirping. Where the rock circle had been were the thin walls of a tall canvas tent, at the center of which smoldered the remains of a fire. In place of the darkness, midday heat and orange light glowing through the fabric surrounding me.

I looked around and realized I was alone.

Something was burning. Not inside the tent, but outside. Or at least it smelled that way. Meat roasting on a spit? No, that wasn't right. This smell didn't stir my appetite but repulsed it. I crept toward the heavy canvas flap wavering sluggishly in the breeze. My walking felt impaired, stunted in some way and when I looked down to check my feet, I got a bit of a shock.

They weren't my feet. The skin showing through the sandals was the color of the outside of an almond, a few shades darker than I'd managed at my tannest. I checked my palms and the gashes were gone. This wasn't my body. I suspected I knew whose it was, though.

I pushed forward through the tent flap, and pain, suffering, loss, and loneliness formed a toxic cocktail of grief in my stomach and a knot like a fist in my throat as I gazed out at the field ahead of me where many of the tents similar to mine were bathed in thick flames, billowing smoke so dark and thick, I thought it might block out the sun forever before long.

The bodies on the ground had met a similar fate, and I ran back into the tent to escape the brunt of the smell.

Family, friends, neighbors—all dead.

I didn't know who did it, but it didn't matter.

"Was this what happened to you?" I asked.

Yes replied a voice in my head.

"And then what?"

I blinked and suddenly my wrists and ankles were in shackles, and I was hurrying across sand, struggling to keep up with a cart while trying not to over extend my steps and trip on the chains. Whoever was driving this cart wouldn't stop, I knew that, and I would end up dragged behind, unable to right myself again.

I tried to speak, but my mouth was too dry, and the sharp inhalation caused my arid throat to seize, sending me into a coughing fit that had no foreseeable end.

"Keep up!" Shouted a voice behind me, I turned to see a soldier in a red uniform behind me, snarling like he was just waiting for an excuse to thrash me.

I quickened my pace, taking tiny rapid steps, sharp pain radiating from my ankles through my calves with each step. How much longer could I go?

Wind kicked sand into my face and I began coughing again. I'd never been so thirsty in my life. The sensation was maddening.

I'm so sorry, I thought. *I'm so sorry this happened to you.*

The moment the thought took shape, I felt a separation inside me, a loosening.

And then I got angry. No, not angry, enraged. She'd already been enslaved in her lifetime, and if that weren't enough, she had two little twerps conjuring her from the afterlife to do their bidding. That made her a slave in the afterlife as well. Couldn't a girl get a break?

Tell me how to help.

"Nora!" shouted a voice.

Who was Nora? I struggled to turn my head to look around, but saw no one out of place when I did, just the caravan of other people like me, chained and transported behind carts, soldiers in red following closely behind, whips at the ready.

"Nora! Push her out!" That voice again.

Was this Nora person in labor? Why would she—

Oh. That's me.

I shut my eyes—Ba's eyes—and felt warm hands on my shoulders. I needed to separate myself from her.

Though part of me felt guilty for leaving her, I knew it was necessary if I were ever going to give her the peace she had more than earned.

When I opened my eyes again, the world was a mix of two realities overlaid. I could still see the desert sand, the prisoners, the soldiers, but I could also see the dark tunnel of trees.

And Donovan.

I'd never thought I'd be so happy to see him.

He lifted me to standing and guided me back to the fire, where he took my hands, completing the circle again. I couldn't help him with the chant this time, but I didn't need to. I could feel it working through me, prying apart the hairline fracture between Ba and me until firelight could flow from it. I did what I could to force her out and into the flames. This was what Ruby had warned me about, that one day there might be a spirit I let in that I couldn't get out, that would try to take me over.

I peeled her spirit away from mine, and the pain was excruciating. And it only got worse when Grim pressed the staurolite amulet against my side. The stone felt like a branding iron on my bare flesh.

She left on the yell that rose from me as I jumped away from the source of pain, breaking the circle with Donovan. The flames sucked Ba into them, pulling her closer then down into them, inch-by-inch.

Ocean spray burst over the edge of the cliff as Ba reached out her shadowy arms for anything she could grab. Part of me wanted to take her hands, to pull her out, but I knew this was the only way she could finally rest.

Then I saw what specifically she was grabbing for in her last desperate attempt. Or rather, who.

"Donovan, get back from there!" He stared hypnotized at the flames and didn't respond. The tips of her fingers curled around the hem of his shirt, and soon he would end up in the fire if I didn't intervene.

Two quick steps, then I tackled him away from the flames, wresting him from her grasp and pushing him out of the stone circle.

I landed on top of him dangerously close to the edge of the cliff. A yard farther, and we might've toppled over.

Donovan pushed himself to his elbows as I rolled to the side of him, both of us staring transfixed at the fire, which crackled, erupted, then disappeared, and with it, Ba.

She was gone, I knew that much. I hoped she'd moved on to a plane where she could find peace and never be summoned again. She had earned that much through her unnecessary suffering.

With the orange glow gone, the realm around us lit only by moonlight, I knew we were finally safe.

But my heart still raced. I rolled flat on my back to catch my breath and count the stars. As Donovan's wand slid down each of my palms, closing the wounds, I shut my eyes against the stinging pain that came with it. Once it was over, I inhaled deeply and opened my eyes again. But I could no longer see the stars because Donovan blocked my view as he leaned over me.

I knew what was coming, and I did nothing to stop it. I met his gaze, and I wanted it. So help me, I wanted it.

"You almost got yourself killed," he breathed.

"So did you, genius."

His eyes flicked down to my lips. "I wasn't sure if you'd make it back."

My breath hitched in my throat. "Me neither."

When he leaned forward, I met him halfway. Donovan was the only thing on my mind, and in that moment, it felt right. No, more than that. It felt inevitable.

Urgency pulsed through me as we kissed. His hand cupped the side of my face only a moment before sliding upward so that his fingers tangled in my hair. He tightened his grip, pinning me to the ground with his body as he tilted my chin up so his kisses could travel lower, down to my neck.

I couldn't remember the last time I'd felt this wanted, this craved. Tanner's kisses were sweet, passionate, but nowhere near this hungry.

Tanner.

Sweet baby jackalope! What was I doing?

Thinking about ending this before it even got to the good part made me want to cry, but I had to. I'd lost myself temporarily after all that had happened. We weren't even in the same world as Tanner anymore, for fang's sake.

But that didn't matter.

"Donovan—"

"I knew you wanted this, too," he breathed in my ear.

I wedged my hands between us and pressed firmly on his chest until his fingers slipped from my hair. "We have to stop," I said.

He moved away hesitantly, staring down at me, a deep crease forming between his eyebrows. "We don't. Look around you, Nora. There's no one here. Well, except Grim, but he's at the tree line marking everything he can. It's just you and me."

Ugh. Why was he making it so hard to do the right thing? "But we can't. I can't."

He listened intently. "Tanner? That's fine. He doesn't have to know."

"Donovan," I said sharply.

"You're not officially together. And this is exactly why. You may have built up your walls, Nora Ashcroft, but you built a door, too, and you left it wide open for someone like me to walk right through."

When I didn't respond, he finally moved off of me with a heavy sigh. I stood immediately, trying to shake off whatever had come over me.

Donovan stood too, blocking my path away from the cliff's edge. "You think I want to hurt Tanner? He's my best friend. But, god, Nora, I want you so bad, and I have for so long, and I know that, deep down, you've felt the same. I know that because I *actually* understand you. Tanner doesn't. He sees you as this incredible mystery to be solved, and once he solves it, you know what will happen."

"Shut up," I said, pushing past him. I stopped by the remains of the fire to gather the supplies into the canvas bag. I slipped it over my shoulder, and when I stood again, Donovan was there in front of me.

"You know I'm right. But I've already solved the mystery. I know you. I understand you." He ran his hands up my arms. "And I'm still here."

Gaia help me, what he was saying resonated.

Tanner always stared at me like I was a puzzle to be solved, and while that made me feel incredible, it also left me terrified. One day, Tanner would discover I wasn't all that complicated, and he would stop looking at me that way. And then what?

While Tanner's kisses were sweet and curious, Donovan's were something else entirely. He knew what he was doing and where he was going. He had nothing to solve.

I could no longer meet his eyes. "Donovan, I know you're right."

I shrugged his hands off my arms and hurried toward the gateway back to Eastwind. *"Grim, let's go. You can't possibly have any more left in you. Not after your stunt in the Deadwoods and Ba sucking all moisture from your body."*

He lowered his hind leg a few yards off from the tunnel. *"Don't tell me what I can't have, Nora. That tree just got the most memorable drop of urine in the history of this realm. Not a single thing had marked it ahead of me. Not one! Ha!"*

At least one of us was in a good mood. He trotted past me, disappearing into the darkness of the bent trees, and I followed slowly afterward. Donovan would come when he was ready. I didn't have the right to hurry him. Not now.

He was ready sooner than I expected, and my lungs felt like they were filled with lead when I heard his footsteps behind me in the darkness.

I kept my distance through the quiet space, though not so much that I could no longer hear him behind me, hear his breathing, the crunch of sticks underneath his feet. I didn't realize until later that it was Donovan and *only* Donovan who occupied my thoughts during that trek back to the Deadwoods.

When I spied the opening of the tunnel up ahead, a fog of bad judgment overtook me in that impenetrable gloom, and I planted my feet, listening to each of Donovan's footfalls as they drew nearer. I turned and waited.

He didn't seem surprised when my outstretched hand found his arm, he simply slowed to a stop. Neither of us said a word. Though I couldn't see his features, I didn't need to. His body drew me to him. There was no resistance between us, whether because our connection spells had removed it or something more was at play, I couldn't tell, but I didn't care. I had to do this.

One last time.

He pulled me tight against him, and I worried I might lose myself in this tunnel, that even if I left, part of me would always remain behind here.

I won't lie, the thought of taking his hand and dragging him back the way we came into that moonlit clearing, only reemerging in Eastwind once neither of us could walk, crossed my mind.

Over and over again.

But I'd already made a decision. This was the last time. Maybe it wasn't fair to him to do this. Maybe it would give him hope he couldn't use.

Old Nora didn't care. And after all, it was her who wanted Donovan more than air.

I pulled back from the kiss when his roaming hands hinted he was about to take it to the next level.

"I'm sorry," I said. I backed away and took a step toward the end of the tunnel before his hand gripped my wrist and whirled me back around.

"If it weren't for Tanner, you would, though, right?"

I think it was the long-simmering rage, the years of hurt I heard in that single question that made me lie.

If I hadn't met Tanner and was single and looking, Donovan and I wouldn't be having this conversation. Our mouths would be preoccupied in other ways back on the edge of that cliff. And maybe in the woods. And maybe back at his place.

But honesty was not the best policy here. Honesty

would put a strain on his and Tanner's relationship that might be the last straw. I couldn't take myself *and* Tanner from him. What I was about to do felt cruel, but I knew it was the best of two terrible options. "No," I said. "Even if I'd never met Tanner, the answer to this would be no."

"I don't believe you," he said quickly. "I know exactly what you're doing, and I don't buy it."

"Maybe you should, Donovan," I replied firmly, pulling my wrist free. "For everyone's sake."

As I emerged from the tunnel, Grim was waiting for me. Something large and dark stirred in the bushes to our right, and when Grim's hackles didn't immediately rise, I surmised that our agreement with the hellhounds was still in good standing.

"Wasn't sure if you'd died in there," Grim said, *"or if Mr. Cheerful mauled you again."*

"He didn't maul me."

"Then what was happening out on that cliff?"

"You know what was happening. Don't make me spell it out. Speaking of cliffs, how much steak do I owe you to keep you from telling Clifford about what happened? And Monster, I suppose. If Tanner ever found out—"

"None," said Grim. *"The beauty of the Deadwoods is that it's full of secrets. You can create all the new ones you want while you're in here and then leave them behind when you go."*

I stared dubiously at my familiar where he padded along next to me with a slight pep in his step, undoubtedly a few pounds lighter than when we entered the woods hours before. *"You're kidding. You aren't going to leverage this?"*

"Leverage what? The fact that the appallingly

palpable sexual tension between you and Donovan finally came to a boil after a near-death experience? Nah. Not today. Frankly, I'm glad you got it out of your system so I don't have to watch it anymore. And so that I don't have to spend any more time around his pretentious familiar."

"I'm glad you're happy," I replied.

"Also, I think we both learned an important lesson today."

"And that is?"

"Donovan is definitely not gay."

Chapter Fifteen

Leaving the cover of the Deadwoods, there wasn't a question in my mind about where I would go next. It was a beacon up ahead, pulling me in with the comforting smell of grease and the flashing *Open* sign.

"*I've never been so thirsty in my life,*" Grim groused.

"*Imagine how the hellhounds feel. It'll be a while before Acher Lake is full again.*"

"*Nuh-uh. You're not gonna make me feel sorry for those dumb slobs. Also, at least there was some water flowing in, even if it was soaking straight into the ground. It's nice when things actually work out. One heavy rain, and the hounds will be right as ... well, right as rain.*"

Donovan had remained twenty or so yards behind on the long walk back, and I tried not to let guilt eat at me for it. He hadn't pushed me about the lie, though. Maybe he would let it be.

I should have felt more relieved. I knew that. We'd figured out who had conjured the drought demon, I'd gotten to smack one of the perpetrators in the side of the head, which had felt incredible, and we'd managed to banish—and hopefully free—Ba. Everyone had survived, so no harm done.

Okay, *some* harm done.

The late-night crowd filled almost every booth at Medium Rare when I pulled open the door, letting Grim run ahead of me.

I shuffled in, bone tired, the spot on my side where Grim had placed the amulet still smarting.

The place went silent.

Oh wow. Did I look that bad?

I scanned the restaurant for him. Bryant was working his regular shift and looked up from his spot behind the counter. That wasn't who I wanted, though.

Finally my eyes found him. He stood next to a booth in the corner where Ansel Fontaine and the redheaded dwarf I'd met briefly at Sheehan's sat together. Whatever conversation they'd been having before I wandered in had stopped short.

Tanner's mouth fell open slightly as he rushed forward. "Nora, are you okay?"

"Yeah, I'm fine."

He grabbed my shoulders, holding me steady as he looked me up and down. "You're covered in blood."

Oh right. That. "It's nothing," I said lamely. "I'm fine."

The bell tinkled behind me, and I didn't have to turn to know who it was.

Tanner's mouth fell open even wider as he stared over my shoulder. "*Donovan*? What the spell happened? Why are you both covered in blood and dirt?"

I could already see it, how the gossip would circulate

from one town busybody to the next. *Nora and Donovan showed up at Medium Rare in the middle of the night looking like they'd just murdered someone with an ax. I heard they were out in the Deadwoods. What were they doing out there? Alone? They're both single, aren't they? I have a guess what they were doing.*

I'd give them something else to gossip about then. Something that didn't require guesswork.

I grabbed Tanner's face in my hands, turning it toward me. My lips had hardly found his before he was all in, his arms around my waist, pulling me closer to his warm body. He didn't mind the blood on my shirt or the mud on my face or the tangles in my hair (caused mostly by his best friend's fingers, unfortunately). He simply held me against him and kissed me back.

It took a lot to shock the late-night crowd at Medium Rare, but this did the trick. Around us were startled reactions from those who hadn't had a clue, and mixed in with that, Ansel muttering, "'Bout time. Jane's gonna keel over and die when I tell her what she missed."

After a night of danger and uncertainty, of doubting myself, not knowing what I wanted, and almost making the wrong choice, I knew, in a way that was rooted in my bones and my blood, that this was right. This was safe. Tanner was the only choice I could have made, in the end.

Let him figure me out. I was ready for it. If he thought he was going to get rid of me anytime soon, he was wrong. So very wrong.

When we came up for air, his eyes were glued to me and full of wonder. Considering the way events had unfolded over the last couple minutes, I couldn't blame him for being taken aback.

Then his eyes jumped to Donovan. "Hey, where are you going?"

My stomach clenched, but I held tightly to Tanner as the bell above the door rang again and I knew Donovan was gone. And not just from Medium Rare.

"Kiss her again, you idiot!" shouted Hendrix Hardy from the back booth.

Tanner laughed along with the rest of the restaurant as he stared into my eyes. He was so beautiful with his soft pink lips, his sprinkling of golden facial hair, and hazel eyes that somehow remained honest despite the hardships of his life. And he was mine.

"Bad news, Nora," he said. "I think our secret's out."

Relief bubbled up my throat and I laughed, even as my eyes start to water up. "I hope you don't mind."

He cradled my face in his hand, running a thumb across my bottom lip. "I've been waiting for this moment since the second you walked through that door four months, three weeks, and six days ago."

And when he kissed me next, the applause and cheers from the customers—our friends and neighbors—felt like an earthquake, shaking the foundations of who I used to be, tumbling my ancient walls to the ground.

Epilogue

"Thanks for coming with me," I said, squeezing Tanner's hand in mine as we made the short walk from Ruby True's house to the library in the early July sunlight.

He shot me a sideways glance. "It's my obligation as your boyfriend."

"Not the most exciting of your duties, but I appreciate it all the same."

Six days had passed since the encounter with Ba in the unknown realm, and I had yet to tell Tanner much of what had gone on. For one, it involved me making a lot of dangerous and reckless decisions, which I knew he hated. But also, a good portion of it revolved around kissing his best friend in a moment of poor judgment. Okay, *two* moments of poor judgment.

I hadn't seen Donovan since we left the Deadwoods and he'd stormed out of Medium Rare. And that was a huge relief. I needed time to just enjoy Tanner and forget about all the jumbled feelings that had preceded my moment of clarity.

"I heard there's this new conveyance in Avalon where you sit inside it and it takes you from point A to point B all while spraying you with cool mist," said Grim. "I bet the grims there don't have to hoof it around town all day in the July sun."

"From what I've heard of Avalon, they probably don't even let grims into the city. You've survived summers before. You can do it again."

"I'm telling you, it's entirely unnecessary for me to go today."

"Is not," I said. "This is official Coven business. You'll be a member of the Coven with me. Ergo, you need to be here."

"It's not official Coven business. It's just you meeting with that Bridgewater boy while Tanner plays chaperone."

"You don't think he trusts me with Oliver?"

"Nope, and for good reason, even if he doesn't know the specifics."

"I thought you said what happened in the Deadwoods stays in the Deadwoods."

"I did. And I'm not saying anything. Just making an observation."

"I can't believe you're trying to shame me after the way I saw Monster cleaning you with her tongue the other day."

"You and Mr. Nice Guy clean each other with your tongue every time I turn around. At least my situation was for the sake of hygiene."

"Look," said Tanner, pulling me out of my mindless conversation with Grim. "It's Donovan."

"Speak of the handsome devil," said Grim.

My heart thudded rapidly, making breathing difficult as I looked around and spotted him up ahead.

He had his back to us as he knelt in fresh earth beside none other than Duncan and Tybalt. I'd heard about this arrangement, but as part of purging Donovan from my system, I hadn't inquired into the specifics.

"Hey, man!" Tanner shouted as we approached.

Donovan turned as he stood and a cloud of unreadable emotions passed over his face when his eyes landed on Tanner and then me.

I quickly let go of Tanner's hand then realized how awful that was and grabbed it again. He and I weren't a secret anymore, especially not to Donovan.

"Hey, Tanner. Nora."

"Can't believe they gave you two doofuses wands," Tanner said, addressing the teenagers.

Nodding, Donovan said, "Special circumstances. Trust me, I tried to convince the Coven that if they really wanted to teach them a lesson, they should force them to replant half the greenery in Eastwind by hand, but they insisted it would take too long without wands. And since they're obviously East Wind witches, I was the best bet to gently guide them off the path of stupidity and make sure they don't try to conjure up any other gods."

"Nice of you to offer," I said.

Donovan twisted his head toward me for a second, his expression like a brick wall, before smiling at his best friend again. "I better get back to it. I want them to finish up here in time to start at Whirligig's today ... mostly because I know Ansel won't be as kind with them as I have to be."

"I'll leave you to it," Tanner replied. "See ya."

"See ya, Tanner."

I didn't bother saying goodbye because it was clear Donovan wanted to pretend I was never there in the first place.

"Cold-blooded," said Grim.

"I probably deserve it."

"Not even a little bit. He's a pretty witch and you're not perfect. The fact that you exercised poor judgment solely because it felt good makes you far more tolerable in my opinion."

"I don't know whether to be grateful that you support me or offended that you think I'm only tolerable."

"For the record, I don't give a jackalope's antlers which you settle on. Believe what you want."

Oliver was waiting with the paperwork at the table closest to the front doors of the library, and he hurried over as we entered.

"Hey, Nora. Good to see you alive." He stopped short of us and shivered when a library ghost walked straight through him. "I heard you were recently covered in blood and who knows what else, so, um, glad you see you're back to normal."

"Yep," I said. "Me too."

"Me too," added Tanner.

Oliver addressed Tanner finally. "How's it going?" The men shook.

"Pretty well, just thought I'd tag along. Hope you don't mind."

Oliver snuck me a quick glance, and I shrugged an apology. "Yeah, that's perfectly cool," he said. "Why don't you three follow me over here and we can look over the amended agreement from the Coven?"

As Oliver briefed us on the arrangement, I discovered it was as boring as I'd expected it to be. "Ruby will be your assigned mentor, since, well, there aren't any other Fifth Wind witches in Eastwind, and I'll be administering your exams and providing supplemental tutoring on some of the basics for the alternative certification that Ruby has no interest in teaching. All sound good?"

"Yep. Then what?"

"Well, as you test out of the various courses that witches are required to take, you'll be awarded different privileges until—"

"When do I get to use my wand?"

He chuckled, mistaking that for a joke, it seemed. But I was serious. "Oh, um. Not for a while."

I cringed. "Ooh, yeah, that's not gonna work for me. Ezra said he'll have it ready in about a week. Rush delivery after the whole covered-in-blood thing."

Oliver leaned forward, head cocked to the side. "Come again? *Ezra* is making you a custom wand before you've *started* formal Coven-approved schooling? Ezra Ares?"

I shrugged. "Yeah, it's legal, right?"

"Technically, yes. But it's extremely unwise. He should know better. How'd you convince him to do that?" He leaned closer. "Money? You must've paid him a fortune."

"No," I said, trying not to be offended. "Ruby asked him to and he did."

Oliver's gently parted lips snapped shut and he sat up straight. "Ah. Yes, that makes sense."

"I didn't realize it was a big deal."

"No, it's probably fine." Oliver clearly didn't want to talk about it anymore, and I wasn't sure why, but I let it go. "As I was saying, once you've earned credit for each course, you'll have to pass the Mancer Trials. Usually, this is right around the time a witch discovers his or her wind, but since you've got that down pat, you should be just fine."

"What are the Mancer Trials like?"

He frowned. "I can't really talk about them."

Tanner nodded at me. "I'll tell you about them later."

Oliver's eyes went wide. "Um, no, you won't. You know that's not allowed."

Holding up his hands in surrender, Tanner said, "All right, all right. I won't tell her." He leaned toward me and whispered, "I totally will."

Oliver clearly heard but steadied himself with a deep breath. "*Anyway*, once you pass the Mancer Trials, you'll be an official member of the Coven and are free to use your magic as you see fit. Within the legal limits, of course."

"You make it sound like so much fun," I said. I reached for the stack of papers and pulled it toward me, spinning it around so I could read it. "What's all this?"

"Terms, conditions, waivers ... mostly waivers. That front sheet is your basic registration form with a questionnaire. It's intended for a much younger applicant, to be fair."

I skipped to the middle of the page and read off one of the questions. "Have you ever intentionally engaged in magic prior to applying for Mancer Academy?" I pretended to think about it, squinting at Tanner. "I don't know. Probably not, right?" I looked suddenly to Oliver. "Does channeling a spirit count?"

Oliver laughed uncomfortably. "You're kidding, right?" When I shrugged noncommittally, he deferred to Tanner. "She's kidding, right?"

"No, sir. Honest as death, this one." His warm hand found my knee underneath the table.

"Do I need to fill this out now?" I asked, staring at the thick stack of paper.

"If you don't mind," replied Oliver. "Then I can take it right back to the Coven and they can start processing it."

I looked at the first line of the registration form and wrote my name in the blank.

"Oh, and before I forget," Oliver said, reaching into a messenger bag over his shoulder and pulling out a single folded sheet of paper. "I grabbed one of these, too. You usually don't fill this out until much later, but, well, special circumstances."

I grabbed it and laid it flat on the top of the stack. "Familiar registration form."

"No way. I'm not going in some database where they can track me."

"Where who *can track you, Grim? You're being paranoid."*

"First name? Grim." I wrote it in the blank.

"Not my real name."

"It is. You didn't have a name until I gave you one. That means it's your real name."

"Last name—" I paused, looking to Oliver. "What do people usually put here?"

He shrugged. "Their own last name."

"Hmm ..." I narrowed my eyes at Grim. "Grim Ashcroft?"

"I would rather die again," he said.

"Ooh!" I set the pen on the line and wrote Grim's new last name.

Tanner leaned over to read. "Grim Goodboy? Hey, that's perfect!"

"You did not," said Grim.

"I did."

Tanner leaned over and scratched behind Grim's ear, murmuring, "There's a good boy. Oh, yes, Mr. Goodboy, huh? Who's a good boy?"

Grim's eyes rolled back into his skull as he moaned helplessly and pushed his head toward Tanner's hand for more pressure. *"Oh sweet baby jackalope. I'm a good boy. It's me! Please make it end ... Good Gaia, I hope this never ends ..."*

Already I was regretting the joke, so I pointedly ignored the weirdness happening next to me and continued scribbling responses on the main questionnaire.

Just a few hundred more pages to get through, then I was officially going back to school.

End of Book 3

QUESO DE LOS MUERTOS
Eastwind Witches 4

Eastwind's annual cook-off seems like the ideal place for Nora and Tanner to finally reveal Medium Rare's top-secret appetizer to the town. But it's never that simple for Nora, is it?

Before she knows it, her secret recipe has turned into a recipe for disaster. Ghostly disaster. And she's the only one qualified to clean up the mess ...

Nora's mysteries continue in
Queso de los Muertos

Grab your copy at
www.eastwindwitches.com/4

About the Author

Nova Nelson grew up on a steady diet of Agatha Christie novels. She loves the mind candy of cozy mysteries and has been weaving paranormal tales since she first learned handwriting. Those two loves meet in her Eastwind Witches series, and it's about time, if she does say so herself.

When she's not busy writing, she enjoys long walks with her strong-willed dogs and eating breakfast for dinner.

Say hello:
nova@novanelson.com

Made in the USA
Middletown, DE
28 September 2023

39657319R00125